Alex's S

CW01508043

Ingredients:

- 1 bottle of red wi
- 1 or 2 green apples
- 1 orange
- 1 peach
- ⅓ cup sliced strawberries
- ½ cup brandy
- ½ cup orange liqueur (you can also use orange juice if you'd like)
- 3 cups sparkling water
- Your desired amount of ice

Directions:

First, cut the fruit into slices and place them into a large pitcher. Save a few slices for garnish! Then, pour the brandy over the fruit. Once that's done, add the orange liqueur (or orange juice) and bottle of wine and stir. Cover the pitcher, and put it in the fridge for at least 4 hours. That way, the flavors can all blend and soak into the fruit. Once ready to serve, add the sparkling water, stir, then pour in a glass of your choice with fresh fruit slices and your desired amount of ice. Enjoy!

Silver Foxed

By Kayla Grosse

This book is a work of fiction. Names, characters, places, and incidents are either the product of the author's imagination or are used fictitiously.
Any resemblance to actual events, locales, or persons, living or dead, is purely coincidental.

Copyright © 2024 Kayla Grosse

All rights reserved. No part of this book may be reproduced, distributed, or transmitted in any form or by any means, including photocopying, recording, or other electronic or mechanical methods, without the prior written permission of the copyright owner, except in the case of brief quotations embodied in critical reviews and other noncommercial uses permitted by copyright law.

To request permissions, contact the author at

www.kaylagrosse.com

Published by Kayla Grosse

Printed in the United States of America

First US Edition: May 2024

ISBN: 979-8-9870546-6-6 (paperback)

ASIN: B0D2N3RVSZ (ebook)

Cover Art Spicy: Mel (IG: @mellendraws)

Cover Design: Kayla Grosse

Edited by Melissa Frey

Formatting: Nicole Reeves

To those that desire to be filled up and
satisfied by a sexy Silver Fox...
This one's for you, my dirty girl.

Author's Note

Dear Spicy Reader,

This book is a super spicy age gap novella. You can expect more spice within these pages than plot (though there is quite a bit of that, too!). To break it down, here's what you'll find:

Age Gap
Dad's Best Friend
Dad's Employee
Heavy Breeding Kink
Dirty Talk
Anal Play
Toy Play
Role Play
Mentions of Pregnancy
Mentions of Getting Pregnant
Rough Sex
Insta Lust

If you'd like a full list of triggers and tropes, you can visit my website: www.kaylagrosse.com for more. As always, take care of yourself and your mental health.

Now, if you're still here (I hope you are!), turn on the Silver Foxed playlist, make Alex's Summer Sangria, and get ready to play house with Alex and her Silver Fox.

Xoxo,
Kayla Grosse

Silver Foxed Playlist

"Fly" Sugar Ray
"Foxey Lady" Jimi Hendrix
"Hey Daddy" USHER
"Cool for the Summer" Demi Lovato
"Movement" by Hozier
"Earned It" The Weeknd
"My Little Secret" Xscape
"Baby, Let's Play House" Elvis
"Watermelon Sugar" Harry Styles
"Into You" Ariana Grande
"Cruel Summer" Taylor Swift
"Can't Get You Out of My Head" Kylie Minogue
"Missing You" Tyler Hilton
"Just the Way You Are" Bruno Mars
"Adore You" Harry Styles

CHAPTER ONE

Alex

"You got my set of keys for the lake house, right, honey?" my mom asks over my car speaker.

"Yes, I stopped by your house on the way out of town and got them from your new housekeeper."

"Oh, yes! Her name is Janie. She's lovely, isn't she?"

I smile to myself. "Yes, Janie is lovely." Truth is, I don't have enough information on Janie to know if she's lovely, but she seemed nice for the ten seconds I met her when I grabbed the keys to my parents' lake house from her early this morning. But that's something I've always admired about my stepmom. She thinks everyone is lovely. It's part of her charm.

While Stephanie Martin tends to be vain and cares more about this season's fashion trends than anything else going on in the world, she doesn't have a mean bone in her body. And most importantly, she loves my dad and me, and she has since the moment she came into my life when I was five years old—which is good enough in my book.

"Honey, I'm so glad you agreed to go to the lake house. It doesn't get used enough, especially considering how busy your dad has been this summer."

I gaze out the windshield of my car and admire the landscape of Starlight Haven, California. This place is probably my favorite in the entire world. Which is saying a lot since my parents have always loved to travel. I've been all over the world, but Starlight Haven always feels like coming home. The mountains, the clear azure lake, and the dense forests—it makes me feel as if I'm living in some fantasy world.

"I'm glad, too; I've missed coming here."

I can hear Mom smile through the phone, probably thinking of all the times we spent together up here while I was growing up. Hiking, biking, hanging out at the beach—it was an amazing part of my childhood.

"Are you almost there? I know you left early this morning. It's such a long drive for only a weekend!"

I put my blinker on and turn into the long tree-lined driveway that leads to the house. "Yep, pulling in now."

"Oh good, good. Are you sure you don't want to stay longer?"

I can hear in the tone of her voice what she actually wants to say: *Are you sure you don't want to stay longer? It's not like you have anything going on in your life besides work, honey,* but she would never say that to me. She's too nice. Not to mention, she thinks I'll start crying. Joke's on her, though, because at this point, I'm all cried out. No more tears are left inside my body. Of that, I am sure.

In fact, this weekend, I have decided I'm not allowed to cry. Only rest and relaxation for me. With maybe a little bit of self-reflection. Why? Because as soon as I get back from my weekend getaway, I'm entering my hot-girl badass-bitch era.

"Unfortunately, I can't stay longer. Allie will kill me if I miss any of my thirtieth birthday week. She wants to meet up every day and celebrate. She's decided it's a whole week affair."

"Oh, yes, yes. I remember you telling me about that. You should've had Allie come up to the house. There's plenty of room."

As the massive lake house nestled amongst pine trees comes into view, I hold back a laugh at how much of an understatement that is. My dad owns a global creative media agency, Spark Life Creative—one of the best and biggest in the world. And while Dad has kept himself relatively humble, he loves to splurge on real estate.

This lake house, or should I say lake mansion, is one of his most prized possessions that he claims he had to fight another man over. Especially since at the time, it was a newly renovated mid-century modern home that used to be the summer getaway of popular singers from the '50s and '60s. This house is gorgeous, to say the least. And my parents have always taken good care of it.

"Thanks, Mom, but I'll be fine. I wanted some alone time this weekend."

"Alright, you know I worry. I'd never be able to be in that big house all by myself."

I clench my jaw. "Why would you say that? Now I'm going to be paranoid!"

"Sorry, sorry! Just be sure to turn on the security system."

"That doesn't help!" I chuckle.

"I shouldn't have said anything. You know it's safe up there, so don't be scared." She pauses. "Oh! Don't forget the stores there close early. Did you bring food?"

I look in my rearview mirror at all the grocery bags. I love to cook, and part of my self-care mission this weekend includes making all of my favorite dishes. It's a bummer they'll only be for one, but I try not to think too much about how freaking single I am. And the fact that, at this moment, I shouldn't be single.

"Honey, are you still there?"

"Yeah, sorry. I stopped at the store on the way in, so I don't have to leave if I don't want to."

"Good, good. Let me know if you need anything else, okay? Your dad and I are going to a charity event this weekend, but we'll be around."

"I will," I say as I pull up to the garage. I use the clicker Janie gave me this morning, and the door opens. "If I don't talk to you, I'll see you later this week at my birthday dinner."

"Sounds good, honey. Love you."

"Love you, too."

The phone call ends, and I turn off the ignition before staring at my green eyes in the rearview mirror. I have my long red hair pulled up into a high ponytail and no makeup on so I can see the patterns of freckles across my face. With all the time I plan on spending at the lake and pool this weekend, I'll not only go through a gallon of sunscreen, but I'll probably leave with twice the freckles. Something my ex-fiancé would've commented on.

He claimed he liked my freckles but always made it seem otherwise. For my birthday last year, he bought me the ugliest straw sunhat to wear with a massive brim, claiming it was "fashionable" and would keep the sun off my face when we went for walks or out together during the day. Fashionable, my ass.

I shake my head to clear my thoughts of him. "Nope. Nope. We're not going to think about stupid Sean!" I yell out loud, my cheeks turning strawberry red from the force of my voice. "You're leaving here a badass bitch, Alexandra Martin. An even hotter, ready-to-have-some-fun badass bitch."

With my mantra now playing in my head, I get out of the car, ready to start my self-care weekend.

Chapter Two

Elijah

I'VE NEVER BEEN ONE for the outdoors. Yet I find myself parked outside a lake house of all places in a town called Starlight Haven.

It's...quaint. Okay, it's more than quaint. The town I drove through to get here is, but this house is—ostentatious, to say the least. I don't even have to go in to know the inside is decorated to perfection. Though I would expect nothing less from Oliver's wife.

Ping!

I slip my aviators over the neck of my T-shirt and unbuckle my seatbelt, pulling my phone from the charger to find one new text waiting for me.

> OLIVER: You make it there alright?

> ELIJAH: I'm arriving now.

> OLIVER: Enjoy your weekend. Remember to relax. I don't want to hear from you or see you online at all. No work, or I'll fire you.

The corner of my mouth turns up in a grin as I type out a response.

ELIJAH: You'd never fire me.

OLIVER: Then I'll give you all our problem clients. I hear Deb is looking for a consult.

I bristle when I see the name of my ex-wife on the screen.

ELIJAH: You wouldn't.

OLIVER: I would.

ELIJAH: …

OLIVER: Like I said, I'd better not see you online. Don't even look at your email. Nothing. Take one weekend off. You deserve it.

ELIJAH: I'm going to HR with this text chain.

OLIVER: I'll say it wasn't me. They'll believe me because nobody thinks an old man like me can text.

ELIJAH: You just outed yourself.

There's a long pause before his text comes through.

OLIVER: Elijah Astor…

OLIVER: Take the damn weekend off. I'll talk to you on Monday.

I grumble a curse under my breath before I type out FINE in all capital letters like a petulant child. While I know Oliver is messing with me, I wouldn't put it past him to make me suffer a consult with my ex if I don't follow his instructions. He's a good friend and boss, but for a fifty-five-year-old man, he sure is meddling.

With my phone now off, I reach for my brown leather messenger bag I had placed on the floor near the passenger seat and slip my phone inside. Did I go against Oliver's blabbering and bring my computer? Yes. But not for the reason he would think.

If I'm going to take a weekend away from work, I may as well spend it doing something I love. Writing. And not copywriting for work, but creative writing. Something I haven't been able to do in a long while considering how busy I've been.

Ever since Oliver made me Vice President of Client Relations last year at Spark Life Creative, I feel as if I haven't been able to breathe. While the money is nice, and I enjoy the travel, I'm tired. I know it's not Oliver's fault, and his convincing me to come to his lake house for the weekend was his attempt to get me to maintain a work/life balance. But I haven't wanted one.

Since my divorce from Deb, I purposely took more work than I should and offered to travel globally when needed. Not only does it soothe the part of me that is a complete control freak, but most importantly, it takes my mind off the loneliness I feel. How at forty-five years old I have everything people dream of—a secure, well-paying job, good friends, a full bank account, and a robust retirement fund—but nothing I would truly call achievements.

I thought by now that I'd have a family, maybe have started my own business or published a few novels. That I would have something to leave behind when I die, something to be proud of. But if I were to keel over right now, my tombstone would read:

Elijah Michael Astor

He was a nice guy with a good job. People liked him.

As my father would say if he was still alive: *How pathetic, son.*

With that lovely thought in mind, I get out of my sports car and stretch my tall body, my knees popping and back cracking as I do. I probably should've rented a better vehicle for the long drive and mountain terrain up here, but summer is winding down, so I decided against it. I opted instead to drive the seven hours from Los Angeles with the top down and the wind in my hair, enjoying the weather.

I'll never admit it to Oliver, but it was nice to finally use my car for what I initially bought it for—joy rides—though my friends all like to joke it was a midlife crisis purchase. Maybe they're right, since I bought it last year after my divorce.

With a sigh, I open the small trunk and grab my travel bag, slinging it over my shoulder while holding my messenger bag in my other hand. Then I study the front of the house.

It's massive. Oliver wasn't kidding when he said I would love this place. While I would never buy a mansion, I can appreciate the mid-century architecture. It's sexy, sleek, and unique.

Feeling a little more excited about the idea of hanging out alone in an expensive home where I can write and enjoy the quiet out of the city, I walk up the stone drive and look at my watch. It's just after six in the evening, which means there's still a couple of hours of daylight left. Oliver said there's a hot tub in the backyard that overlooks the lake and private beach. He also said the sunsets are unreal. And while I don't like the outdoors,

I do enjoy hot tubs and nice patios with a good view. Especially if a glass of wine is involved.

My stomach growls, and I'm reminded I haven't eaten since breakfast, a matter I should take care of before I drink wine and end up getting drunk alone. However, at this point, that sounds like it could be a good idea. I need to do something different to get myself out of the monotonous routine I'm in.

With my evening now officially determined, I fish out the key Oliver gave me and insert it into the lock of the massive multi-paneled mahogany door that probably cost more than my mortgage. When the interior is revealed to me, I let out a low whistle. This place is...beautiful. That doesn't seem like the right word, but it's the only one I've got right now.

Once I've closed the door and locked it behind me, I set my bags down and look around, taking in the whole space. The floor plan is open, seamlessly connecting the different living areas. There are large floor-to-ceiling windows and glass doors that allow natural light to flood the spaces, which are decorated with sleek furniture and minimal art. While I haven't seen the house in its entirety, from what I can see, the space feels homey and inviting.

More excitement fills me at the prospect of spending time exploring this place like a museum, studying all the clean lines and geometric shapes. I know Oliver's wife likes art, too, so I bet there are some beautiful and rare pieces in here.

I rub the back of my neck, chuckling to myself at how giddy I just got. But I can't help it. I enjoy the simplicity and functionality of things. I'm also a sucker for homes that are made of sustainable materials. It's one of the personality traits that Deb never appreciated nor cared for in the ten years we were married.

I let out a grunt. Why did Oliver have to bring up my ex? He wants me to be relaxed this weekend. But now I'm irritated thinking of her and our excruciatingly long, drawn-out divorce that was made final this past year. A milestone I haven't had time to fully celebrate yet. Maybe I'll toast to that while I'm in the hot tub tonight.

Thump!

The soft and sudden noise has the hair rising on the back of my neck. I stay still and try to attune my hearing toward the origin of the noise. For a moment, I think I imagined it—or maybe something in the home was settling—but then I hear another noise, almost like a clanging. Followed by another soft thumping noise.

If I was rational, I would get out of the house and call the police to come investigate. But this is a small town, so I doubt the cops would get here quickly. It's more likely that an item fell over, or an animal got in, especially in a big house surrounded by forests and mountains. And there's a part of me, the overly confident part, that says I can handle myself against an intruder. I'm tall, lean, and work out every day to stay fit and active, especially as I get older. I trust that if I needed to, I could defend myself.

When I hear another clanging sound, I pick up my pace, looking around for anything I can grab in case I need to take action. This is when minimalism doesn't help anything. It would be nice if Oliver collected baseball bats or swords.

With a quiet exhale, I clench my fists at my sides, turning a corner to be met with an expansive dining room. I look straight ahead, and I stand there awkwardly when my brain takes in what I see beyond it. The open floor plan does nothing to hide the state-of-the-art kitchen with a panoramic view of the lake beyond. But that's not the view that stops me in my tracks. No, that's not it at all.

It's the naked back and ample round ass of a ginger-haired woman. She's standing at the sink washing a pan in a tiny white thong. Her hair is tied in a high ponytail, the soft waves of it landing between her pale freckled shoulder blades. As I allow my eyes to study her further, I see there's a red string tied around her generous waist, which I assume is an apron.

Fuck me. My mouth goes dry, and my cock stirs beneath the placket of my dark-wash jeans as time freezes and my brain stops working altogether. When she starts humming a tune I don't recognize, it's as if my trance deepens, and I can't help but admire the rest of her. My eyes make their way down and up the curves and lines of her bare, full-figured thighs before settling on her flared hips.

I swallow, my tongue like sandpaper against the roof of my mouth. I should be a decent man and make myself known. I should let whoever this insanely sexy woman is know that she's not alone in the house.

As I debate my options for the best way to handle this, I pray that she doesn't turn around. Because if she does, I have a feeling this will not end well for me. Unless Oliver hired her? No. I shake my head. He wouldn't do that. If he did, he'd at least warn me. He's the type of friend who tells you too much information, not less.

Maybe if I cover my eyes and clear my throat, she won't be as afraid? Or I suppose I could just turn around and walk back the way I came, and she'll be none the wiser that I was even here, ogling her like a pervert. Yes, that's what I should do. I should walk away. With my decision made and my gentleman brain coming back online, I start to turn on my heel.

That's when I'm met with a blood-curdling scream.

Chapter Three

Alex

There's a man in my house. There's a fucking *man* in my house. From what it looks like, a very sexy man. But a man that I do not know is *in. My. House*! Okay, my parents' house, but sort of my house. Oh my god, I'm freaking out. I am *freaking out*.

I scream again as I press my bare ass against the cool sink, using my arms to try to wrangle my boobs that are falling out from the sides of the too-small apron. At least I was smart enough to put it on in the first place. Not that I thought a man would show up to find me mostly naked, but I didn't want to get oil burns.

Why the hell am I thinking about oil burns? A stranger is *in my house*.

I open my mouth to scream again, but he holds up a hand. "Please don't scream," his warm voice pleads. "I swear I'm not going to hurt you."

My eyes dart from his large palm to his salt-and-pepper beard and perfectly styled silver hair. Then I do the thing he asked me not to do—I scream then grab the first thing I see: a wooden spoon. I hold it up and stare at the stunned man in the dining room, glad there's at least some space between us.

"Who the fuck are you?!" I yell, my question a high-pitched screech.

His stunning blue irises that remind me of the lake stare into me, unblinking. I shake the wooden spoon at him and try to ignore the way his penetrating gaze sends a zing straight to my lady parts.

"Hello! I asked you a question. Who are you?"

His attention travels from my face to the wooden spoon, the corners of his lips tilting up slightly before he looks back at me. He shifts on his feet, and I wave the spoon at him.

"Don't come any closer! Answer me; who are you?"

He holds up both his hands and doesn't move, his eyes still trained on mine. At least he's keeping his gaze on my face instead of my almost naked form.

"My name is Elijah. I'm friends with Oliver Martin, the owner of this house."

My dad has friends? I mean, of course he has friends. And I guess this attractive silver fox is his friend. But I've never heard him talk about an Elijah. I repeat his name again and again in my mind, but I don't know any Elijahs.

"How do you know him?" I ask, confused.

"I'm the Vice President of Client Relations at Spark Life Creative."

Elijah. Vice President of Client Relations. I repeat it again and again until it finally clicks. My body flushes pink when I realize who he is.

"You're Astor?"

The man nods, his perfectly angled jaw flexing along with the well-developed lean muscles in his arms that he has clenched at his sides. "Elijah Astor," he confirms. "Oliver likes to call me by my last name. But we're close friends. He gave me access to this house for the weekend. I swear, I'm not going to hurt you."

My body still tense, I gently lower the spoon and place it on the counter, crossing both my arms over my chest to give me more coverage. "My mom said it was going to be empty this weekend."

I watch Elijah's brow pinch as he processes my words and drops his head back to look at the ceiling. His mouth moves silently as if he's praying or maybe he's cursing. When he drops his head down to his chest, I hear him ask, "Are you Oliver's daughter, Alexandra?"

"Yes, I'm Alex." This time, I do hear him curse. For a moment, he doesn't say anything. I watch his chest move up and down in heavy breaths, the muscles of his biceps ticking beneath the fabric of his fitted gray T-shirt. "Elijah?" I ask when the silence becomes too much.

"I'm sorry, I should go. This is highly inappropriate," he says, his tone tight and eyes on the ground.

A smile tugs at my lips. *This is highly inappropriate* I want to mimic back in a British accent, but I don't. I find it amusing that he sounds so proper for a man who looks like he does, someone who'd take you over his knee and call you a bad girl. Not a man who averts his gaze and apologizes for doing nothing wrong.

He turns to leave, taking a few steps forward with his hands still clenched at his sides. I don't know why, but I find myself going after him. "Wait!" I call.

As if he forgets the reason he turned to leave in the first place, he spins on his heel to face me. But as soon as he sees my apron-clad form, he spins back around.

"Sorry," he apologizes again.

"It's fine. Let me go put something on. Don't leave." Before he can say anything, I rush out of the kitchen and up the stairs to the master bedroom. Breathing harder from my efforts, I untie the apron and lay it on the California King before grabbing the first thing I see in my suitcase. I pop the emerald sundress over my head and tug it down. It's a skimpy thing with thin fabric and a short hemline that I'd normally wear over a bathing suit, but it will have to do for now. I'm in a rush to get back downstairs.

Why? I don't exactly know. But I don't want to keep Elijah waiting. I have a feeling if I left him down there long enough, he'd leave without a word. I want to at least talk to him about what happened so he doesn't tell my dad about this. It would be awkward as hell.

Once I've slid on a pair of underwear with more coverage, I'm running down the stairs. When I don't see Elijah in the dining room, I panic. I hear the jingling of keys and rush to the front door, completely out of breath now.

When his tall form comes into view, a nice duffle bag over his shoulder and a leather messenger bag in his hand, I frown. "I told you not to leave."

He tenses at my voice and turns, his sapphire gaze looking me up and down. It's hard to tell if he likes what he sees because his bowed pink lips are pursed and his forehead is still pinched. Not that it should matter. I shouldn't want this man to like what he sees, right?

"This is your family home, and I'm intruding," he says. "I'll go find a hotel for the night and head back to LA in the morning." When he grasps the doorknob, I jump into action, placing my hand over his. My fingers touch the skin of his knuckles, and static electricity zips up my hand. We both gasp. I pull away and shake it out.

"Are you okay?" he asks quietly, those damn blue eyes boring into mine as if he's genuinely concerned that I'm hurt.

I shoot him a small smile. "Dry mountain air."

He nods, standing to his full height in front of me. My head hits the upper part of his chest, and my skin prickles from how close we're standing. I tuck a loose strand of hair behind my ear and take a breath in an attempt to calm my fast-beating heart. It doesn't help that Elijah is a very attractive man.

From far away, I could see he was good-looking, but up close? Holy wow. With a jaw that could cut glass, high cheekbones, a well-manicured beard, and not a single hair out of place, this man could be a model. And now that I can see his face more clearly, I'm going to guess he's not as old as I initially thought. Probably quite a few years younger than my dad. Which excites me more than it probably should.

Elijah swallows, his Adam's apple bobbing in his stubbled throat as his gaze darts to the V of my dress. I have large boobs, so anything I wear that has a lower neckline will show cleavage. But the longer he looks, I realize that, in my rush, I forgot to put on a bra. My nipples go hard under his attention, and I cross my arms over my chest.

Elijah clears his throat and glances down at his watch. He's flustered to the point that I can see a tinge of pink on the apples of his cheeks.

"I should leave before it gets dark," he says.

I reach out and take his bicep in my hand. The skin is warm under my touch, and I swear he shivers. "Sorry," I say, pulling my hand back and giving him space. "Just stop trying to leave."

I laugh lightly.

"I don't understand how my parents double-booked us here, but you're here already. And you're my dad's friend. You can't stay at a hotel."

"It's fine. It will be one night."

"The hotels are probably booked," I counter. "It's their busiest time of year. I doubt you'd be able to find one. Just stay here for the night. It's totally fine."

"I should at least try to call and see."

I press my lips together, wondering if I should be offended that he's so determined to leave. Though my rational brain understands why he wants to.

"If you feel like you need to, go ahead. Though it's really not a problem for you to stay here. I bet if you text my dad, he'd insist you stay, too. He wouldn't want you to waste your money when we have plenty of perfectly good rooms here."

Elijah looks at his bags and then back at me. "Are you sure? I don't want to make you uncomfortable."

"I promise you're not. But if it makes *you* more comfortable, you can sleep in the theater room downstairs. That's as far as you could possibly get from me and the master bedroom."

His eyes soften. "Please don't take my wanting to leave the wrong way. This is"—he makes a small gesture between us—"complicated and awkward."

I twirl a piece of my wavy hair around my finger. It doesn't escape me that Elijah watches the movement with interest. As if my body has a mind of its own, I pop my chest out a bit so his attention wavers back to my cleavage before he quickly looks into my eyes. Could this man really be attracted to me?

I paint a warm smile on my face and cock my hip, placing a hand on it. "This doesn't have to be complicated. Or awkward. Stay the night, and if, in the morning, you still want to leave, feel free."

Elijah swallows again, and I'll admit I love the way his stubbled throat flexes and the veins in his neck pop as he does it. *Wow, Alex,* I internally scold myself. Maybe I should drive thirty minutes across the Nevada border and go to a club. Apparently, I'm horny and need some attention. If I didn't, I wouldn't be actively eye-fucking my dad's friend-slash-employee. But I mean, who can blame me? This man is gorgeous.

Finally, after what seems like forever, he stops the war he's having with himself and nods. "If you're really okay with it, I'll stay for the night."

"Oh, great!" I clap my hands and do a silly little excited jump. Elijah's eyes go straight to my boobs at the motion, and I bite my lip to keep from smiling. I know I shouldn't, but I like that he's looking. I like that it seems our attraction to each other is mutual. Even if it's a little naughty given who we are.

"Thank you for offering," he says, "but please let me know if at any time you want me to leave."

I let out a breathy laugh. "That won't be happening. As you said, it's only for the night. And really, Elijah, no thanks needed. Though I wouldn't suggest sleeping in the theater room, especially when we have perfectly good beds."

He chuckles, and I'm relieved to hear the sound. "A guest room sounds wonderful."

"Then follow me! I'll show you where they are." I grin at him, moving toward the staircase that leads upstairs. He smiles back as he shifts his bag over his shoulder, then he falls in step behind me.

Chapter Four

Elijah

WHAT IN THE HELL am I doing? What. In. The. Actual. Hell.

That's all that is running through my mind as I walk behind my best friend's—and boss's—daughter. And staring at her ass, no less. The very plump ass I saw framed by a thong and gawked at for far too long. The perfectly round-shaped ass I will now dream about.

Jesus. I'm going to hell. If Oliver knew about this, he'd kill me.

"Do you like darker colors or brighter ones?" Alex asks, the dulcet tone of her voice going straight to my groin.

I clear my throat in an attempt to get a grip on myself. "A mix of both."

She looks over her shoulder at me with those big green doe eyes of hers. My god, she's beautiful. And far too young. *And off-limits,* Oliver's voice says in my head.

"Hmm. I thought you were going to say darker."

"Why is that?" I ask, genuinely curious. She slows her step a bit so we're almost side-by-side as we walk down a long hallway on the top level of the house.

"I know we just met, but you're so serious." She giggles a bit.

The sound is so sweet and melodic, it doesn't help the semi I've been trying to control since I saw her almost-naked freckled body in the kitchen. It also doesn't help that her choice of dress leaves little to the imagination. When we were downstairs, it took everything in me not to reach my finger out and trace the perfect circle of her nipples through the thin emerald cotton.

I clear my throat again. "I'm not that serious."

"Really?" She quirks a light-red eyebrow at me as she stops in front of a bedroom.

"I can be very unserious if I want to be." The words I'm saying are true, though her assumption is right. I am normally a serious person. But given the right environment and people, I let myself relax.

Lately, though, that side has been harder to bring out. Another reason Oliver told me to take a break.

Alex hums but doesn't say anything. I want to ask her what she's thinking, but she gestures for me to walk through the open door.

"Ladies first," I tell her.

She smiles, her round freckled cheeks naturally pink. "So formal."

I open my mouth to answer that it's called being a gentleman, but she walks through the door and into the bedroom. She twirls around in a circle with her hands out, the motion flaring the hemline of that too-short dress so that I see the tops of thick thighs.

"Do you like it?" she asks, her hands still out, gesturing to the room.

I want to say, *Yes, I like it. I like it too much,* but I wouldn't be talking about the bedroom. My jaw clenched, I set my bags down and look around the room.

The decor is typical of a mid-century modern home. The king-size bed is low to the ground and covered in a thin taupe comforter with a gray blanket folded lengthwise at the bottom to accent it. There's also a matching gray bench seat that appears to flip up for storage at the base of the bed and an abstract painting hanging over the walnut headboard.

"It's nice," I say honestly. "It's a great mix of light and dark."

Her smile beams, and I realize in that moment that even if I hated this room, I would say I loved it just to see her smile like that for me.

"Oh, good. The bathroom is through there." She points behind me. "And that is the walk-in closet." She points next to the bathroom. "If you need help with the shower at any point, let me know. I haven't been here in a while, but I think I remember how to operate all the fancy buttons."

Lewd images of me taking her wet nude form from behind, that perfectly curved ass of hers slapping back into my pelvis repeatedly, flashes behind my eyelids so quickly, I feel as if I've been hit by a freight train. I press my eyes shut, and when I open them again, Alex looks concerned.

"Are you okay? You're flushed."

I manage a tight smile. "It was a long drive up here." That fact is true. I am tired and hungry from the drive. Though that's not why I look peaky. Thank god she can't read my mind, or she would've called the cops on me by now. Hell, I should call the cops on myself.

"Oh! I'm so sorry." She smacks her forehead, and I have the desire to grab her hand and kiss the skin she just hit.

I dig my fingers into my thigh—I've lost my goddamn mind. Maybe I should've seen a psychiatrist instead of taking a vacation.

"What are you sorry for?" I ask, my voice, by some miracle, sounding normal.

"I'm a terrible host. I should've at least offered you something to drink."

I think of how we met and picture her serving me a glass of water in that apron. I clear my throat and shift on my feet. "You weren't supposed to host me. No apologies needed."

"So my dad offered the house to you for the weekend?" she asks, sitting down on the bench seat.

I try not to cringe when she calls Oliver "dad." It sobers me a bit to hear her say it, reminding me she's off-limits and my thoughts are still highly inappropriate. "Yes, it was very last-minute," I say, sticking my hands in my pockets.

She hums, tucking a loose tendril of hair that looks like silk behind her ear. "So typical that my dad wouldn't ask my mom before offering the place to you. She thought it was going to be empty this weekend. We didn't have any rentals on the schedule."

"Like I said, I'll stay the night then leave tomorrow. Then you can continue on as if I was never here."

Her light laughter fills the air. "You made a memorable entrance, Elijah. I don't think I'll be able to forget your visit, no matter how short."

With that, she pops up off the bench and takes a step toward me as I try not to let the images of her naked ass in that white thong pop into my mind yet again. "I bought a ton of groceries. If you'd like to get settled then come down to the kitchen, I'm making chicken cacciatore for dinner. I was also planning on breaking into my dad's wine cellar. After all this, I could use a drink."

"That's kind of you." My mouth is already watering at the idea of a home-cooked meal. When was the last time I had one? I can't remember.

She smiles. "It's no trouble. You came here to get away like I did. Or at least I'm assuming you did. If you insist on leaving so soon, you might as well get a night of relaxation in before your long drive tomorrow."

"Alright," I say, knowing it's probably a bad idea to be anywhere near her. But I do need to eat.

"Great," she says excitedly. "I'll see you downstairs."

Alex spins and walks toward the door, the late sunlight from the windows streaming in to catch strands of golden brown mixed in with the orange and red hairs of her ponytail. In her swift departure, I'm left with a lingering scent of rose that tickles my nose and goes straight to my groin. I adjust myself and walk to the door, closing and locking it before I rest my head on the cool wood.

I shouldn't have said yes to dinner and just starved for the night. But I couldn't help myself. She's so damn beautiful, and apparently, I'm a glutton for punishment.

After another inhale and exhale, I walk to the bench seat, sitting in the exact spot Alex just was. I reach for my phone and turn it on. As it powers up, I debate if I should text Oliver, let him know what happened minus walking in on his daughter mostly naked. But instead, I find myself opening a search browser on the internet.

While I knew Oliver had a daughter, I surprisingly don't know much about her. I think the last thing I remember him saying was that she was always so busy with one thing or another that he and his wife hardly ever saw her.

Curious to know her, especially after our meeting, I type "Alexandra Martin" in the search bar and press enter. Immediately, several results appear for her. I know it's the same person because her picture pops up beside the name.

I click the first link, a networking website, and discover she's a first-grade teacher at a private school in Los Angeles. That explains why I've never seen her around the office, then. Not only does she not work for Oliver, but I know teaching is exhausting, especially elementary school. Or at least that's what I've heard from friends of mine who work in education.

Images of her teaching play behind my eyelids, and I smile. Even though we've just met, her personality is warm and open. I bet she's a wonderful teacher.

Going back to the search, I scan the page for my next click. When I see one for a local newspaper in Los Angeles, I stop and click as soon as I see the headline:

Alexandra Martin Engaged to Business Mogul Sean Jamison Jr.

My stomach bottoms out. Alex is engaged? I could've sworn she was flirting with me before. But maybe she was just being nice and I'm simply reading into things because I've been lonely. And because I'm attracted to her.

I furrow my brow as I try to remember if she was wearing a ring, but I don't remember seeing one. Come to think of it, neither Oliver nor Stephanie ever mentioned Alex getting engaged or that she was dating anyone. My curiosity grows as to why my friend would leave something that large out of our conversations.

I study the black-and-white picture of the couple and wonder if it's because Sean Jamison Jr. looks like a total smarmy asshole with his perfectly coiffed brown hair and clean-shaven jaw. The article is over a year old now, and I highly doubt they ever got married. Because if my best friend left me off his daughter's wedding invite list, I'd wonder if we were really friends at all. Which I know isn't the case.

I also doubt she'd be on a weekend getaway by herself to a remote home her parents own, cooking mostly naked, if there was a man in her life. And if there is, that man needs to get his head examined because I would never let a woman like her out of my sight.

My cock twitches in agreement, and I release a long sigh before I stand from the bench and turn off my phone again. After I drop it on the dresser, I open my travel bag to grab a fresh pair of clothes. I think a quick shower is in order because there's no way I'm going to make it through dinner without doing something I'll regret, like asking Alex to sleep with me. Or coming in my pants. Both of which would be mortifying. Both of which I cannot allow myself to do. Hopefully, my fist can take the edge off, and I'll be able to have a nice, normal dinner with her.

Yes, that's what I will do. I'll ask her questions about her life instead of stalking her like a creep online. I'll get to know her better, make small talk, and then I'll leave in the morning. No harm done.

I'll let my attraction be only that. An attraction.

CHAPTER FIVE

Alex

I'M POURING TWO GLASSES of red wine as a freshly showered Elijah walks into the kitchen. He's barefoot now in dark-wash jeans, wearing a similar-colored denim button-up with the sleeves folded below his elbow and the top few buttons left open. My eyes go straight to the smattering of dark chest hair peeking out, and I have to stop my mouth from falling open.

Holy mother of God.

Elijah smiles as he approaches me, completely unaware that he's set my panties on fire. Scratch that. He's melted them.

"It smells wonderful in here," he says, looking over my shoulder at the food I have simmering on the stove.

"Thanks," I say, sliding a glass of wine toward him. "I hope you like Chianti. It's from 2016."

He lets out a low whistle. "You sure you want to share this with me?"

"Isn't there some rule that you have to share expensive wine with someone?"

"Not at all."

I smile coyly. "Fine, but at the end of the day, who really wants to drink alone, right?"

Elijah's serious blue eyes stare into me as if I've said something that struck him deeply. "Right," he says after a moment. I'm wondering if he drinks alone often. By his reaction to my words, it would seem that he does, and that makes me sad. Because while Sean and I parted ways over six months ago now, I am not alone. I have my best friend, Allie, our group of girlfriends, and my family.

Now I want to know who Elijah has or doesn't have. I don't see a wedding ring on his finger, and I can only guess he doesn't have a girlfriend because he came here alone like me.

I hold up my wine glass, deciding this man needs to have a little fun. Even if he only stays one night, I can give him a night of company. Even if it's platonic. Because let's be honest, if he is interested in me like I think he is, I doubt it will go any further than harmless flirting. Which is sad—I bet Elijah is wonderful in bed. He gives off that big dick energy without even trying. And he seems like a sweet guy.

"Cheers," I say as Elijah holds up his glass. "To an evening of not drinking alone—and good company."

The light tone in my voice has the corners of his mouth tugging up. He repeats my words back to me before he clinks his glass against mine. We bring our drinks to our lips, and our eyes stay connected while we sip the savory liquid. His gaze is strong and steadfast as he swallows, and I feel like the moment happening between us right now is erotic.

I swallow my wine and then avert my gaze, knowing that if he keeps staring at me like that, I can't be held liable for my actions. Setting my wine glass down on the island, I feel his eyes follow me as I go to check the dinner. I grab a potholder and lift the lid on the cast-iron skillet, the hot steam wafting up. Elijah is right; it does smell amazing. Happiness fills me as I admire the rich and rustic dish I've created. The chicken is falling off the bone, which means it's ready.

"Do you need help with anything?" Elijah's velvety timbre asks, making the hairs on the back of my neck rise. I pick up the wooden spoon and turn around to face him.

"Nope, it's ready."

Elijah's eyes track from my face to the wooden spoon I'm holding. When his attention settles on me once more, he's blushing again. I know he's thinking about earlier.

A playful smirk forms on my lips. I shouldn't like that my dad's friend is clearly thinking about me naked, but I can't help it. I do. It feels nice to be desired, even if nothing comes of it.

"You know, a wooden spoon could've been a great weapon," I tease.

A burst of laughter shoots forth from Elijah, and something inside me changes at the sound. It's wonderful. I want to hear him laugh again.

"What would you do with it?" he asks.

I hold the spoon in my one hand then tap my chin. "Hmm. I suppose hitting you with it wouldn't do much. But I think if I had chucked it at your head hard enough, I could have potentially poked an eye out. Or at least stunned you enough to get a head start." He laughs again, and the tingling warmth I feel in my belly spreads throughout my entire body.

"Maybe next time, reach for something sharper."

"Are you suggesting you'd rather I'd come at you with a knife?"

His blue eyes turn serious. "I want you to be safe."

A lump forms in my throat. Who is this man, and where the hell did he come from? We don't know each other, but I one-hundred-percent believe that he would've accepted me coming at him with a knife had it been in self-defense. Maybe it's because I'm his friend's daughter, but I get an odd feeling it's more than that.

"Good thing I'm safe with you, then," I say honestly.

His self-assured gaze falters for a split second, but then he smiles gently. "Good thing."

Chills zip up my spine, and my toes curl against the hardwood floor. I decide it's time to eat—otherwise, we'll stand here all night saying weird things to each other while I try to figure out if he's into me or if he just wants to take care of me because he knows my dad.

"Will you take our wine to the dining table?" I ask. "I'll plate everything up and bring it over."

"Of course." He picks up the broad-based glasses dutifully as I turn my focus to the chicken cacciatore. After I have everything plated how I like, I walk it slowly over to the way-too-beautiful man sitting at the table.

He watches my every move as I set the food down in front of him. I try to ignore how it feels, how every part of me tingles with his focus on me like that, but it's hard to do. So once the food is out of my hands, I head to the kitchen to grab a salad from the fridge I'd made earlier and take a deep breath. When I arrive back at the table, Elijah is eyeing his dinner plate like it's the Eighth Wonder of the World.

"Go ahead, eat," I tell him as I take the seat at the head of the table with him to my right. I smooth out my purple-colored skirt of the sundress I put on and place my napkin over my lap.

Elijah looks up from his plate, and in place of his intense gaze is pure excitement. "This looks beautiful."

"It's nothing," I say, reaching for my fork.

As I pick it up, his hand covers mine. "It's not nothing," Elijah says.

I stare at his warm hand over mine, the veins prominent as he squeezes. Without thinking of it, I flip my hand over, and our palms meet. To my surprise, he takes the offering and holds my hand with steady pressure as I look at his handsome face.

His smile is sincere and gentle as he says, "Really, Alex. I can't remember the last time someone cooked for me. Thank you." Then he pulls back his hand, and I'm left staring at my now burning palm, feeling as if he marked me somehow with that simple touch and his gratitude.

"You're welcome," I reply quietly, trying to get it together. I grab my wine and take a sip, hoping the alcohol can knock some sense into me.

There is no reason for me to be so attracted to Elijah. He's my dad's friend, for one. He also works with him.

And there's the little fact that he's older than me, though that doesn't really matter. I've always said that if people are consenting adults, they can do what they want. But I know my dad would take issue with it.

I dated a man in his mid-fifties once, when I was twenty-five. Dad hated it, and I get why from his perspective since the man was close to his age. But that relationship was stable and fun. We didn't work out in the end because we had different plans for our lives. He already had children and didn't want more. I, on the other hand, knew I wanted babies. That desire has only grown as the years have gone on.

Sean's face enters my mind for a split second, and I take another sip of wine. Nope, we're not thinking about him. Or any of my exes, for that matter. Not when I have a man who I think is single in front of me. Because I for sure have already double-checked for a ring, and there isn't one.

I give my full attention back to Elijah as he brings a forkful of food to his mouth, his eyelids closing as his lips wrap around the metal of the fork. I don't miss the small smile that tugs at the corners of his mouth as he chews.

When a gentle moan reaches my ears, the tips of them turn pink, and I swear a bolt of electricity hits my clit.

"You like it?" I ask, my voice breathier than I expected it to be.

He savors the flavor of it for another moment before opening his eyes. "'Like' is an understatement. It's the best thing I've ever tasted."

I think I go into a full-body blush. Something I can't hide because of my fair skin, a trait I've been told I inherited from my mom's side of the family.

"That can't be true. If you're friends with my dad, you've been to the best restaurants in the city. Maybe even the world."

At the mention of my dad, Elijah seems to tense a bit, and I make a mental note to mention him as little as possible. Especially since I want to explore this buzzing attraction between us.

"Oliver does have expensive taste. But I prefer meals that are made with love. And this," he says with conviction, pointing his fork at his plate, "has been made with love."

Yep, I've definitely turned the color of the tomato sauce. "That's really nice of you." I exhale, trying to calm my blush. "I've been so busy I haven't had the chance to cook recently. But I do love it. Especially when I can cook for other people."

I take a bite of my own food and let out a little groan myself as the rich sauce hits my taste buds.

Elijah clears his throat and shifts in his chair. "What have you been busy with?" he asks, sounding genuine. "If you don't mind sharing."

I shake my head and swallow. "No, not at all." I take another sip of my wine as I think of how to answer this question. "I was engaged until about six months ago. We broke it off, which created a lot of chaos."

"How so?"

I grab the open bottle of Chianti Elijah brought to the table and refresh my glass. His is still mostly full, so I set the bottle back down then take another long drink.

"You don't have to say if it upsets you, Alex."

I express appreciation for his thoughtfulness with a soft, grateful smile. "It doesn't upset me."

Elijah brings his attention to the wine in my hand, and I huff a light laugh.

"It's more annoying than anything, really," I continue. "Sean and I weren't compatible in the end. So we broke it off. And while we hadn't started doing much wedding planning, the breakup caused a ripple effect in our social circles." I put my wine down. "But that's boring and stupid. The bigger issue was that we lived together so I had to move. Do you know how hard it is to find a place that isn't infested with roaches at a reasonable price in Los Angeles?"

Elijah swallows his bite of food, his brow pinching like I've noticed it does when he's thinking. Even when he's not doing it, I can see the fine lines on his forehead from his years of scrunching. I want to reach out and smooth the skin with my thumb. Thankfully, I have some self-restraint.

"I have to say I haven't had to look for a place in a long time. But I've heard the market is bad," he says.

"I live on a teacher's salary, so finding a place in my budget near my school isn't easy, either."

Again, Elijah's brow pinches. He opens his mouth as if he wants to say something, but then he closes it again.

"What is it?" I ask.

He sets his fork down and wipes his mouth. His blue gaze penetrates mine again. "Forgive me if this is rude, but I would think Oliver would be glad to help you."

I grin. The question doesn't offend me. I've grown up with privilege and get asked questions like this all the time.

"He would," I say, warming at all the times my dad has slipped money into my account only for me to return it. "And trust me, he's wanted to. But after I graduated college and got my first job, I refuse to take his money. I like to buy my own things, pay my own way. That was something Sean and I argued over a lot, too."

I stop myself from getting angry thinking of the arguments we used to get into. One time, I gave my credit card to the waiter at a nice restaurant, and he was pissed for two days after, saying I made him look like a broke idiot who couldn't pay for his fiancée's dinner. That was one giant red flag that made me start to question everything with him.

"Can I ask you something?" Elijah says, his brow still pinched.

"Only if you promise to relax."

Elijah raises an eyebrow at me. "I am relaxed."

My restraint crumbles, or maybe the wine is hitting my system, but I can't stop myself. I reach across the table and press my thumb into his forehead, against where the skin is scrunched. The whole time, Elijah sits in his chair, his eyes watching me carefully. It doesn't escape me that his breath has picked up at my touch and nearness.

"Didn't anyone ever tell you that if you keep your face a certain way for too long, it will get stuck that way?" I tease, moving my thumb across the textured skin.

Elijah expels a breathy laugh, and his brow finally relaxes. Satisfied, I lower my hand and sit back in my chair. "See, was that so hard?" I ask.

He beams and reaches for his glass, taking a long sip. "Thanks for your help."

I make a silly salute. "Anytime."

With a shake of his head and a long exhale, Elijah's shoulders relax, too. I top off his wine for him after he sets it down, and then we settle back into our meals.

We take a few more bites before I ask, "What was it you wanted to know?"

He swallows his bite of food. "Honestly, this is more of a selfish thing to ask."

"Ooh." I smirk. "Go on."

He chuckles. "Oliver speaks about you quite often, but he never mentioned you got engaged or that you were even dating anyone. I wonder why he never spoke of it."

I chew and swallow another bite of food as curiosity fills me. "Why is that selfish?"

The hand that was bringing Elijah's wine to his lips pauses in midair. His brow almost furrows again, but he stops it. "It's only that your dad and I are close. That is a huge deal in your child's life, and he said nothing. It makes me think we aren't that close."

"Oh, no, don't think that," I answer. "It doesn't surprise me that he didn't say anything. He hated Sean. My dad hates all the men I date." Elijah's brow pinches once more, and I wonder why that made him bristle.

But I soldier on. "Sean swept me off my feet with promises of settling down, babies, all the things I told him I wanted when we first started seeing each other. But Dad suspected from the beginning that he was dating me for some weird status thing and to help get one of his new media businesses off the ground. Dad wasn't very happy when we got engaged, but he went along with it because he thought I was happy."

"And you weren't?" Elijah asks.

I shrug, pushing my near-empty plate away. "I was at first. Or at least I think I was. Honestly, I don't know. I think I was happy with the idea of Sean more than anything. And eventually, from what I could tell, Dad was right. When I started talking about family plans more aggressively, our already meager wedding planning halted altogether. After months of nothing, I finally told him either he wanted a family with me, or he didn't. His silence told me everything, so I broke it off."

Elijah sets his fork down on his empty plate. "I'm sorry, Alex."

"Don't be sorry. Do you want more food?"

He pats his stomach. "If I eat any more, I'll burst. But thank you again. You didn't have to feed me after I intruded on your getaway."

"Technically, we both kind of intruded on each other's getaways."

"At least let me help you with the dishes."

"You don't have to do that."

"It's no trouble. I like doing dishes."

My eyes narrow at him. "You're lying."

A nice smile graces his lips, enough that he shows me his straight white teeth. "It's relaxing. I like the repetitiveness."

"Interesting. I guess we make a good team then, because dishes are my least favorite part."

"Then I'd be glad to help."

"You wash, I dry?" I ask, pushing up from the table.

Elijah stands with me, offering his hand like we're making a gentleman's agreement. "Deal," he says.

With an amused smirk, I put my hand in his warm palm and shake.

"Deal."

CHAPTER SIX

Elijah

WORKING IN TANDEM WITH Alex to clean up the kitchen brings into stark focus a domestic daydream that's almost primal.

It's a simple act, one that's not new or extraordinary but speaks to a part of myself I don't often acknowledge. Or perhaps more truthfully, I haven't *let* myself acknowledge it since long before my divorce, when my marriage with Deb was new and I thought we'd wanted the same things.

I dry my hands on the dish towel as Alex puts away the last of the plates. I allow myself to watch her profile for a moment. She's humming a tune, the low notes soothing any last bit of nerves I had about being in the same room as my best friend's daughter.

While the attraction I've been trying to deny is still there, I've enjoyed spending the last half hour getting to know her better while we've worked as a team to wash and dry the dishes. Unlike me, Alex is an open book. I've asked her about her job a bit more and if she ended up finding an apartment sans roaches. Thankfully, she did. One she's moving in to after her thirtieth birthday next week.

Thirty. I knew she had to be at least in her mid-to-late twenties after seeing her job profile earlier, but finding out she's about to be thirty shouldn't excite me as much as it does. It's nice to know our relationship wouldn't be completely inappropriate.

I clench my jaw. *There is no relationship, Elijah. You're here for one night. Then you'll leave tomorrow and go back to your boring life where you'll work all day and go home to an empty house.*

As Alex folds the dish towel she's been using and turns to face me, I wonder if she feels lonely, too. I related to what she said about getting out of a relationship with someone who didn't want the same things. I also can't deny that what she wants is what I want as well. Expressing her desire to settle down and start a family only added fuel to the already burning flame of my attraction to her.

I'd be lying if I didn't admit there was a part of my brain that already started to picture what it would be like to have a life with her. It was easy to do after she fed me a delicious meal then we did dishes together with the kind of practiced ease married couples have.

Alex smiles at me, her freckled cheeks stained a light pink. A normal occurrence for her because of her fair skin, I've realized.

"Thanks for doing that. I appreciate it."

"It was no trouble."

She moves toward the island where our wine glasses sit almost empty. "Do you have a preference for our next bottle?"

I set my now perfectly folded dish towel on the counter near the sink, making sure it's evenly lined up with the straight edge of the basin before turning back to her. She clearly saw what I'd done, and she's smiling wider because of it but doesn't say anything.

"I should probably call it a night," I say, knowing that if I drink more wine with her, I'll end up forgetting that I shouldn't want my friend and boss's daughter. But when her face falls at my words, I can't help but think that allowing myself to be interested in her and not judging myself for it could really be a good thing.

"It's still fairly early," she says, looking at the microwave's digital clock. "Unless your bedtime is nine pm?" When she finishes her sentence, the tease in her voice is evident. She traps her plump lower lip between her bottom teeth and grins at me.

Maybe Alex is the devil in disguise, here to test my resolve.

"I'm not that ancient," I say, unable to stop myself from grinning back at her. "I simply don't want to intrude on any more of your evening." That last part is a white lie. I most certainly *do* want to intrude on her evening. I also want to intrude on certain parts of her. Certain parts I couldn't help but imagine while I masturbated in the shower earlier, like that lovely ass of hers.

"Oh, hush." She takes a step toward me. "You know you're not. I enjoy your company."

"I enjoy yours as well," I admit.

She sighs a breath of relief that sits like a warm drink in my belly. "Then don't go to bed. I was thinking of using the hot tub, and you could join me. My parents installed a brand-new one with lots of powerful jets. It will help you relax, Mr. Serious."

I chuff, failing to keep images of Alex in a bathing suit out of my mind. "I am relaxed."

Her hand comes up, and like at the dinner table, she smooths the pinched skin of my brow. "Whatever you say, Mr. Serious. But honestly, you have to enjoy a soak before you leave."

One corner of my mouth lifts as she pulls her hand away. "If you insist."

"I do."

I exhale a resigned but amused breath. "Alright, then. I'll join you."

She does the little excited bounce she likes to do, making the tops of her generous breasts jiggle. My cock stirs to life, and I'm hit with the realization I agreed to be in a hot tub with the most beautiful woman I've ever seen. The one I am trying not to be attracted to. God, I'm such an idiot.

"I've already got my suit on under my dress," she says.

My eyes drag down her sundress-clad body like I have X-ray vision. When I meet her green gaze again, instead of blushing or trying to act like I didn't look, I hold eye contact and own what I just did. I think I can at least be an adult and stop pretending like I don't find her good-looking. There's no harm in that, right?

"Why don't you go change and I'll get the hot tub ready?" Her own gaze peruses my body now, as if me ogling her gives her permission to openly do the same to me. Which, in fairness, it does. And I can't say I mind it.

"Sounds good."

She walks past me, our arms brushing as she slips by. The brief sensation sends a shiver up my spine. When I turn to watch her go, she's glancing over her shoulder at me with that devilish grin on her face. "See you out there, Mr. Serious."

When she's out of sight, I turn to the island and adjust myself for what seems like the millionth time in the last few hours. Then I grab my wine off the counter and down the remaining liquid in one gulp. This may be the second-dumbest idea I've had today, the first of which was to stay overnight.

Though the raw excitement in my gut feels as if it's trying to tell me otherwise; that maybe, just maybe, this could be a smart decision.

Well, a fun and memorable—albeit stupid—one, anyway.

CHAPTER SEVEN

Alex

As the cool night air caresses my skin making goosebumps erupt along my arms, I carefully place two fresh glasses of wine on the smooth surface surrounding the sunken hot tub.

I make sure I space them near each other in hopes that Elijah will sit next to me. Is it a cheap move? Yes. But I want to see what he will do. I want to know if what I felt during our dinner together is real or if I'm making it up in my head because I want him to like me. Because I want him to show me what I think I already know: that he's interested in me.

After the way he looked at me in the kitchen just now—and his over-gentlemanly and sweet actions since we've met—I think he is. I'm sure it's weird for him that I'm his friend's daughter. But again, like our age difference, I don't see a problem with it. It's not like I'd met Elijah before this. If anything, the fact he's friends with my dad gives me a little bit of hope, because then maybe he'd like someone I dated.

I pick up one of the glasses of wine I just set down and take a sip. Why am I thinking about dating him? That's insane. Certifiably insane.

I hear the sliding glass door open, and I turn to see the object of my thoughts standing there in all his half-naked glory. He's in a pair of dark-blue swim trunks that almost look black in the porch light. They fit him like a glove, the edges tight enough that they accentuate the corded muscles of his thighs. But that's not what catches my attention.

My mouth goes completely dry, all the moisture in my body going straight between my legs as I trail my eyes up the toned and tight muscles of his stomach. My gaze continues going up his happy trail to his taut chest with the smattering of dark and silver hair I saw peeking out of his shirt at dinner.

That is why you're thinking of dating him, my brain says to me. I internally scold myself for being incredibly shallow. But I know his attractiveness is not the only thing drawing me to him; I feel a connection to him. How I told him about my life at dinner, how nice it was to do dishes together—it felt easy. Right.

Elijah closes the door and takes the few steps needed to get to me, his eyes dropping down my bikini-clad body so quickly I think he was hoping I'd miss it. I do a little cheer inside that he looked then add a point to the bank in my brain that says he's attracted to me.

He smiles, gaze darting to my wine. "What did you choose this time?"

"Oh," I say, trying to pull myself together. "It's a merlot, single vineyard."

He hums. "Notes?"

I take a sip and move it around my pallet. "Black plums, blueberries, dark chocolate..." I taste again. "And vanilla bean."

His brows shoot up, and he nods his approval. "You know your wines like Oliver."

"He taught me. We go to Napa every year together. It's a thing of ours."

"Oh, yes, I remember him saying something about that."

I keep my focus locked on him, trying to get a read on if the mention of my dad made him uncomfortable like before. Thankfully, he seems fine. But I'm not going to test it further.

"Let's get in; it's a little chilly out here," I say.

He holds out his hand, and I stare at it. "I don't want you to slip as you get in."

I press my lips together. "Such a gentleman."

While I would be fine getting in myself, I hold my wine in my left hand and give him my right as I walk the few steps down into the heated water. His grip is strong, and I savor the brief contact before I let go to sit down. I lean back against a cluster of powerful jets and sigh in delight as Elijah joins me, sitting exactly where I had placed his wine. I do another little cheer and add one more point to the "like" side in my brain.

He takes his wine in hand and sips then swallows another one before putting it down. We're sitting close enough that our thighs almost touch beneath the water, both facing the view of the lake. It's too dark to see right now, but if we listen close enough, we can hear the lapping of waves against the shore over the sound of the jets.

"Nice, isn't it?" I ask Elijah after a moment of silence.

"It is." He leans back against the jets with a groan. "It's been a long time since I've been in a hot tub."

"Same. You should see the view during sunset. It's beautiful."

"I'm sure it is," he says, staring at my face. The way he says it makes me think he's not referring to the sunset. If I wasn't already flushed from the hot water, I would blush more.

"So why did you need a break for the weekend?" I ask, not only to spark conversation but because I genuinely want to know.

"According to Oliver, I work too much."

"Do you?" I ask.

He sinks further into stream of the jets, his broad shoulders relaxing into the water. The movement causes our thighs to make contact. My eyes widen at the feeling, but to my surprise, Elijah doesn't try to pull away nor does he apologize. Another point.

"If you would've asked me that on my drive up here, I would have said no," he muses.

"And now?"

He shifts, his muscular thigh sliding against mine. "I'm realizing that Mr. Serious has been out to play for far too long."

My entire body feels as if it's been covered in popping candy. My skin zips and tingles, and my thighs press together as another tiny bolt of lightning strikes me between my legs. Before I can think about what I'm doing, I shift so I'm turned toward him and rest my hand on the top of his thigh beneath the water.

Elijah doesn't flinch at my touch. Instead, he holds eye contact like he does every time we speak. But this time, it's different, darker. Even in the dim light, I can see the desire in his eyes. There's no denying he wants me, too.

"Alex," he says headily, "this is a bad idea." But nothing in his tone or body language says this is bad at all.

"What if I like bad ideas?" I ask teasingly, gently sliding my hand up his thigh. I only stop when my fingers meet the outline of his very prominent erection.

Elijah curses under his breath, but he still doesn't pull away. Instead, his body slips down the hot tub wall so my palm now rests over the very large bulge beneath his swim trunks. I internally pat myself on the back for correctly guessing that this man, in fact, does have a big dick to go with his BDE.

"Alex," he sighs, his voice almost pained.

I cup him then gently squeeze until he groans. "How long has it been since someone's touched you, Elijah?"

He swallows, a long moment passing before he says, "A long time."

I gently grip him again so his eyes roll in the back of his head. "How long?"

"Two years," chokes out.

I try to keep the shock off my face. A man like him hasn't had anyone touch him in two years? I find it hard to believe, but I don't think he's lying. He has no reason to.

I stroke my hand up his clothing-covered cock, brushing my thumb over the thick crown of it. "Can I make you feel good, Elijah?" I rub my own thighs together at the thought of being the first one to touch him in so long, to take him in my mouth and watch this serious, beautiful man come apart for me. To have him grab my hair and use me how he wants.

The filthy images continue to pile on as I wait for an answer. I move closer to his body, the pressure from my hand on his cock increasing as I slide the tops of my wet breasts against his arm.

"Please," I purr into his ear, rubbing my nose along the shell of it. His cock jumps beneath my hand, and I bite down on his earlobe. It may be excessive, but I feel like a woman driven by pure aching need for him. It's unlike anything I've ever felt before.

"I'm going to hell," he groans, "but god help me, yes." His blown-out pupils connect with mine as he says it. "Take care of me, Alex."

That's all I need to close the distance between us, my lips sealing over his in a burning kiss. If he's going to hell, then I'm going to hell with him.

CHAPTER EIGHT

Elijah

ALEX'S LIPS ARE SOFT and pliant like the rest of her and even sweeter than I imagined. I cup her cheek with my hand, sliding it down her neck so I can pull her closer. She moans at the contact, her mouth opening so my tongue can slip in.

As I lick into her mouth for the first time, I'm transported to a different plane altogether. I may be going to hell, but she tastes like heaven. As our tongues tangle in a new dance, I become ravenous, wanting to consume her. Taste every note of her like she did that wine.

"Elijah." She whimpers against my lips as my hand grips the base of her neck while I press my thumb into her rapidly beating pulse point. "I want to make you feel good."

"You are making me feel good," I say, kissing her now swollen lips, not wanting to go another second without her taste.

She moans, and the hand she has on my cock applies more pressure as she rubs those incredible tits on me. My god, I missed this—being with a woman, having another person's hands touching me, pleasing me.

Alex trails her fingers along the waistband of my swim trunks, her nail brushing against my lower abs, causing them to contract.

"Sit up on the edge," she says, pulling away.

I arch an eyebrow at her. She puts her lips into a demure pout that I'm certain would make me do anything she asked of me.

"Please," she says, her fingers slipping beneath to brush over the hair leading to my cock. Feeling conflicted about not pleasing her first but also needing to please her by doing as she asks, I extricate myself from her and sit on the edge. Alex doesn't waste any time, moving in front of me and gripping the top of my shorts.

"Lift up," she says. When I do, she tugs at my wet bottoms, pulling them down enough that my hard length bobs free, slapping against my wet abs.

"My, my, my," her dulcet voice coos, "what a pretty cock you have." As if my penis likes being told it's pretty, it twitches under her praise. Has anyone ever told me my cock is pretty before? No. But apparently, I like hearing it from her lips.

Kneeling on the seat before me now, she runs her fingers up my calves under the water, slowly dragging them up, up, up. Not only do I like the sensation of her hands on me, but I enjoy the way the bubbling jets move the water around her breasts, making the flushed skin bounce as she teases me.

"Pull your top down for me, Alex," I command, letting my desire for her take over. I'm not thinking about anything else but us right now, about what she's offered me. I'm going to make it count—everything else be damned.

She looks shocked for a moment, but then she pulls back from me and stands with a siren smile pulling at the corners of her mouth. The lights from beneath the water light up her body, and I'm mesmerized by the way the water droplets run down the curves of her skin and slip into the valley of her breasts.

The jets kick up water around my calves, and my breath quickens as Alex reaches behind her to undo the clasp of her forest-green bikini top. Once the material is off, she throws it, the fabric making a wet plopping noise as it lands on the ground nearby. She bites her lip then runs a finger down her chest, my eyes tracking the movement. My hand moves to my cock, fisting it while she teases me. He and I are both happy that I can now see her bare, perfectly round, light-pink areolae and revel in how tight her nipples are for me despite the hot water.

"You're touching what's mine, Elijah," she tuts, her voice low and dangerous. "I want to admire you first." I pump my cock up and down slowly while she watches me do it. "Then you can play all you want."

She licks her lips and palms her heavy breasts that are painted with freckles, squeezing them together. More sexual acts I'd like to do with her fill my mind, images of burying not only my face between them but my cock, too.

"Are you wet for me, Alex?"

She nods, pinching her nipples now.

"Will you show me?"

She doesn't miss a beat as she takes one hand from her breast and slips it down into the water, beneath the high waist of her bottoms. She lets out a small moan that goes straight to my straining length as her fingers encounter her folds.

When she pulls them back out, her hands are wet from the water, but I can see the slick arousal there, which means she's weeping for me. Taking my hand from my cock, I remove my trunks the rest of the way and open my legs for her.

"Come here," I request, my voice low. "But don't put that hand back in the water."

She steps forward, her eyes remaining on mine as she offers me her fingers without me having to ask. I take her wrist and open my mouth, placing the wet digits between my lips to suck them clean. A whimper escapes her as she sees me savor the flavor of her. A mixture of the saltwater and her tart pussy explodes on my tongue. When I've gotten it all, I slide her fingers from my mouth and kiss her palm.

"Elijah," she breathes. "Can I please touch you now?"

I suck the pulse point on her wrist. "You want to take care of my cock, Alex?"

"Yes. Very much."

I smile against her delicate skin, leaning back so I can place her hand on my cock. When her soft palm wraps around it, my breath hitches in my throat. I press my hands down beside me to keep my balance, gripping the edge of the tub as she starts to jack me in slow, measured strokes, exactly how she saw me do it myself.

"Does that feel good?" she asks, her eyes never leaving mine.

"More than good," I manage to say. I'm glad I took the edge off earlier in the shower or I would've come from the few strokes of her hand.

Alex shifts, sinking her free hand into one of my thighs before kneeling again.

"Are you comfortable like that?" I ask.

She giggles. "I'm fine, Mr. Serious." Then she bows her head and licks the ruddy tip of my cock, her warm, wet tongue lapping up the pre-cum that's gathered on the swollen head.

"Yes, Alex," I say on an exhale, my head dropping back as my hips thrust up, seeking more. I get my wish as she darts her tongue out again, swirling it around before sucking on the tip and sliding her hand down my shaft.

"God, that feels good." I moan, my chin dropping down so I can watch her every movement.

Her green eyes are staring up at me as her mouth descends on my cock, her lips stretching wide to take my girth. As they slip down, a bead of sweat drips from the crown of her ginger hair as water splashing up from between her bare breasts hits her chin. It's erotic, sensual, and completely and utterly filthy.

Alex smiles with her eyes while she takes the hand on my cock down to cup my balls, rolling them in her palm as she feeds more of me into her mouth. Unable to keep myself from touching her, I take one of my hands and grip the base of her skull, my fingers tangling in her damp hair. Since we've never done this together before, I don't know how much she can take or how rough she likes it, but the way she relaxes her tongue against me gives me the information I need.

"Tell me if it's too much," I say, my voice sounding almost as if I'm an entirely different man, one completely overtaken by his sex drive. One completely overtaken by the incredible woman who's freely offered herself to me.

She hums around me, her nails digging into my thigh as if to urge me on. I place my hand further up on her head, my fingers framing the elastic of her ponytail, then I push her down as I piston my hips upward. My cock disappears further into her mouth before I pull her back up again, the tight skin glistening with her saliva as I work her back down again.

"You feel so good," I moan, slowly fucking her face, not going too hard yet so she can get used to my length and girth. Her mouth is about halfway down when she hollows her cheeks, sucking me. "Yes, Alex. Just like that," I praise.

She hums again and takes more of me on her own. I thrust my hips up harder at the same time, the head of my cock hitting the back of her throat. She gags, her eyes watering.

"Are you okay?" I ask, not wanting to hurt her.

She doesn't pull away to answer; instead, she takes her hand from my balls and runs a finger over the sensitive skin behind them. The action surprises me, as no one's ever touched me there before, but the sensation causes me to buck into her mouth. She gags again, more this time, but she still doesn't falter, swallowing me down as she breathes through her nose.

"Fuck!" I curse as she continues to suck and fondle me. The base of my spine starts tingling, the sensation of my impending release coiling low in my belly. I grab her chin and pull her off my cock, and the string of saliva stretching from it to her mouth almost has me spending all over her face and chest. But I don't want to come yet.

"Elijah," she pouts, and it's the cutest and filthiest thing I've ever seen in my life.

"You're such a cock-hungry girl, aren't you, Alex?"

Her eyes widen, and then a slow and languid smile appears on her face. My hand still grips her chin firmly. "Mr. Serious, you're surprising me. Such a dirty mouth," she purrs.

"You like it?" I ask, feeling slightly self-conscious. My ex-wife didn't like when I talked dirty. She didn't like anything much, for that matter. That's one of the many reasons I haven't been intimate in so long.

Alex licks her lips then moans as if she can taste me on them. "I more than like it. Tell me what you want, Elijah. Tell me exactly what you want me to do to you, how I can make you feel good."

I want to tell her she's already made me feel more than good, but my body and the filthy mind she's unlocked has other ideas. My cock aches as a scenario pops into my mind.

"Are the jets manually adjustable?" I ask, stroking the wet skin of her cheek.

One red eyebrow lifts. "Yes, why?"

"Take your bottoms off. But don't tease me, Alex."

Alex stands and steps back, her freckled breasts swinging as she pushes her bottoms down and off, letting them float away in the water. I can't see her pussy, but I can imagine what it looks like, what it feels like. The desire to touch myself while I admire her beauty is strong, but I manage to keep it together.

"Come here," I say. She moves back, and my eyes are still entranced by her chest, her flushed skin, and her damp red hair that my fingers are itching to pull free from her messy ponytail. "I want your sweet mouth on me, but I need you to get off, too. Do you understand what I'm saying?"

A playful smile lifts the apples of her cheeks, and she nods. I help her get back between my legs. This time when she kneels, she parts her legs wider. Sliding my hand down between our bodies and into the water, I feel around for the jet I want until I reach it. Alex's breath hitches, and when I tilt the powerful stream of water toward her center, she cries out.

"Oh god!"

"You like that, Alex?"

Her hands grip my thighs for balance as I watch her legs spread wider. I chuckle at her enthusiasm.

"I'll take that as a yes." With my hand back on her chin, I direct her mouth to my cock. More pre-cum has gathered at the tip in anticipation of what's to come. "Now open those pink lips of yours, and get me off."

With that devilish look in her eye, almost as if I've challenged her, she licks the pre-cum off then slides my cock down her throat until I hit the back. This time, she doesn't gag as she starts to bob up and down. Water sloshes around us from the movement of her body and the jets, and I bring my hand up to grip the back of her head again. "Yes, just like that, you dirty girl."

My praise has her moving faster as her sharp nails dig into my thighs. My cock twitches in her mouth, and that tingling sensation at the base of my spine comes back. I use my palm to help direct her down and back up. Her moans and whimpers as the jet assaults her pussy get louder, and I know she's close, too.

I thrust my hips up and push her down, her throat relaxing enough that her nose brushes the top of my pubic hair.

"Yes, Alex. You're so goddamn perfect." Her body starts to shake, and her mouth becomes less practiced as she nears her release. "Are you coming, my dirty girl?" I ask, the blunt ends of my trimmed nails digging into her scalp.

She moans a muffled "yes" around my cock, the vibrations almost tipping me over the edge.

"Look at me, Alex. I want to see your eyes as you get off on that jet."

She looks up at me with a wide, glassy stare, mouth full of my cock as I plunge into her warm, wet hole. Her body trembles then tenses right before she shatters. She holds on tight to my legs as she shakes, and I push her head down on my cock, letting the sound and visual of her taking her pleasure while giving me mine bring me even closer.

"You're so fucking beautiful when you come." Alex's eyes remain open, and her cheeks hollow as she gets her bearings again, her body still shaking and her cheeks pink while she sucks.

"I'm going to come," I warn her. But instead of moving off my cock, she holds herself on me, one of her hands on my thigh and the other cupping my balls in a firm grip. With her eyes on me and another suck of her lips, I let myself release.

"Oh, yes, Alex. Oh, fuck," I grunt, cupping both hands around the back of her head to keep her on my cock. She doesn't falter, taking everything I give her. She swallows my release, her throat contracting around me as I spill myself inside her. My cock pulses and pulses as fireworks explode behind my eyes and my orgasm rocks my entire being. In this moment, I know nothing else except her and the sensations in my body.

I don't know how long her lips stay wrapped around me, but when I'm finally spent, I release her. Alex pops off my softening cock, using her pointer finger to wipe a tiny bit of my cum from the corner of her mouth. Our eyes stay connected as she sucks it between her swollen lips, a sated and satisfied smile on her face as she swallows the remaining bit of my release.

Once she moves off the seat below me, I drop down into the water and haul her between my legs for a kiss. She doesn't waste time opening for me, letting me taste myself on her tongue as her hands weave into my hair. The action compresses her breasts against my chest, and she moans as I drag my hands down the soft rolls of her back to rest on her hips.

When she presses her pussy into my lower body, the curls of her pubic hair brush against my skin, and I finally pull back. Her eyes are hooded as she stares at me so sweetly. *Fuck.* I know that if I don't stop this now, I'm going to have sex with her. Then I'll never leave this place tomorrow.

"Elijah," she says quietly, "don't think so hard."

I press my lips together. "I'm not."

She gives me an *Are you joking?* look then rubs her thumb along my brow. "Mr. Serious is back," she teases.

I exhale as she places both hands on my shoulders. With the after-orgasm dopamine drop, the realization of what we allowed to happen between us comes crashing down around me. My body stiffens.

"Elijah." She digs her nails into my skin. "We're two consenting adults. We did nothing wrong."

I blink at her. "How did you know that's what I was thinking about?"

She lets out an exasperated chuckle. "It's not that hard to figure out. I'm having the same thoughts."

"Then why aren't you freaking out?"

"Like I said: two consenting adults."

"Alex," I say quietly. "You know it's not that simple.""It doesn't have to be complicated. I like you, Elijah. I wanted to take care of you. The end."

I swallow the ball that's formed in my throat, the words "the end" making my stomach sour. Does she want it to end? Was this that simple for her? I'm not one to treat any kind of sex as transactional. Especially now, after I've had a taste of her, when all I can think about is taking her upstairs and exploring the constellations of freckles on her skin, the curves and dips of her body.

The hands that I haven't been able to remove from her hips grip her tighter at the images.

Her eyes soften, and a hopeful smile tugs at her lips. "Unless you don't want it to end?"

I tuck a strand of wet hair behind her ear. "I said I would leave tomorrow." The words come out with less gusto than they should have.

"Or you could stay," she offers.

"Alex." Her name is a pathetic whisper on my lips.

"I'll tell you what. We go to bed, and in the morning, if you want to stay, come to my bedroom when you wake up."

"What?" I cock my head, eyebrows raising.

"I know you're stuck on the whole 'me being Oliver's daughter' thing."

My jaw clenches, not wanting to hear his name after I came down Alex's throat a few minutes ago. The two things are just wrong to think about together, and it makes me sick to my stomach. Not because of what we did but because now I feel like I need to go to jail or something.

She sighs. "This doesn't have to be more than a weekend, Elijah."

My curiosity spikes. "What do you mean?"

"We both came here for a reason. To relax, relieve some stress. I don't know about you, but I'm feeling pretty good right now." She smiles.

"Yes, I am, too," I answer. Because despite my thoughts, I do feel the best I have in years.

"Good. Then think about it. We spend the weekend together, we have some fun, then we go our separate ways. My dad never has to know."

"He'll figure it out eventually," I counter, "that we were both here at the same time."

"I'll text my mom tomorrow and let her know what happened. This is a big house. I'll tell her you're staying in the guest room and we're doing our own thing. They'll never think more of it."

"And this ends after one weekend?" I grip her tighter.

That playful, devilish smile turns up on Alex's face again. "Yes."

I contemplate her offer, considering the consequences of one of us catching feelings or of Oliver finding out.

Alex leans forward and presses her naked chest into mine before kissing my chin. "Sleep on it, Mr. Serious. If you want to stay, come to my bedroom tomorrow morning. If not, no hard feelings."

I search her gaze. "You'd really be okay with this?"

"What my daddy doesn't know"—she takes my lip between her teeth—"won't hurt him."

With that, she pulls away and walks out of the hot tub, her delicious ass the last thing I see before she wraps a towel around herself and walks inside.

Not once looking back.

Chapter Nine

Alex

I flip on my stomach and debate if I should get up. The morning sunlight streams through the windows as I slide around on the soft sheets and check my phone again. It's eight thirty, which means it's only been five minutes since the last time I've checked.

I slept a little, but the majority of the night, I tossed and turned. My brain seemed unable to shut off as I kept replaying last night in my head. Elijah surprised me with his dirty mouth, the way he used me, how he got all commanding. I guess I was right that he would be the type to take a woman over his knee.

The urge to slide my hand between my legs and bring myself to orgasm grows. I swear I can still feel the jets on my pussy as he fucked my mouth. God, that was hot—the hottest sexual encounter of my life. The way he made me strip. The way he held my head as he worked me up and down that beautiful cock of his.

I cup my heavy breasts, nipples tight as my body lights up like a tree on Christmas. Just as my hand slips further south, a bird chirping wildly outside stops me. I flop my arms down at my side and try to think of something that won't turn me on. It's still early, and I'm not sure what time Elijah gets up. So I'm still hopeful he'll take my offer. That he'll be the one to get me off this morning.

I prop myself up against the pillows and stare out of the floor-to-ceiling windows that look over the lake. I don't see any boats out, and even if there were any, they wouldn't be able to get close enough to see my naked body tangled in the sheets.

For a while, I gaze out at the blue waters and trees beyond, trying to let the beauty of this place calm me. But all I can think about is Elijah fucking me from behind while I stare out at this view, our reflection in the windows as that cute, furrowed brow of his pinches in pleasure, not stress.

"Ugh!" I clench my thighs together. How has this man gotten under my skin so quickly? I've had one-night stands before, and I didn't feel this way the morning after. I wish that he wasn't my dad's friend and employee. If he wasn't, I think Elijah would've been in my bed last night.

However, he's hung up on it. Which I can understand. But at the same time, what does it really matter?

We don't know each other. We're both adults. Both of us came here for stress relief and time away from reality. And while I'm sure my dad would have different opinions, he doesn't control my life. He doesn't get to choose who I'm with. And like I told Elijah, what my dad doesn't know won't hurt him. This can be a weekend thing. An earlier-than-planned start to my hot-girl badass-bitch era where I take what I want and feel good.

My clit makes its presence known again, and I look once more at the time. It's only been another five minutes. What if he's a late sleeper?

Fudge muffins. Maybe I should've told him a time. What if I'm waiting here for another few hours? Or what if he never comes?

I nibble on my lower lip. He has to come. The way he reacted to me last night, I knew he wanted to say yes. In fact, I felt confident. Though maybe I read the whole situation wrong.

I fix the sheets then stare at the door I left cracked open. I hear no sounds yet. I haven't even heard a cough or a sneeze. Which means he's still sleeping or he left while I dozed off at some point.

I could get up and check, but I don't want to seem desperate. I take a deep breath, trying to practice some calming breaths my mom taught me. She loves her yoga. She's always trying to take me with her, and I went once, but that was enough. Though I can appreciate that yoga does make you bendy.

I'm hit with another onslaught of images as I picture what kind of pretzel positions Elijah could get me in. What would it feel like to have that dick inside of me, moving in and out of my pussy instead of my mouth?

"Screw it!" I get up out of bed and head to my suitcase, opening the pouch where I stowed some sex toys. Since I was going to be here by myself, I thought a little self-exploration would be nice. I'd even gotten some new toys to try, one of which I'm embarrassed I purchased.

I pull out the toy in question. It's a remote-controlled large silicone dildo that looks and feels very much like a real cock. There's even a suction cup on the base so I can stick it to a surface and ride it. But that's not what makes it different, nor does the fact that it vibrates—it's the small hole at the top instead.

My stomach clenches, and I wonder if I'm pathetic for buying it, for buying something that simulates ejaculation.

My cheeks flush. I pride myself in being very open and sex-positive, but I can't help but think this is dumb. That my desire to feel like I'm being filled up is silly. It's not like this thing can get me pregnant. I'd need a real dick and a partner for that, one I'd want to have kids with. One who wants to have kids with me. And my IUD would need to be removed.

I reach back into my suitcase and pull out a bottle of lube and the syringe. I glance at the partially open door again, my heart pounding a little faster. I should wait a bit longer for Elijah to come. If he walks in on me using this, he may run for the hills. What we shared last night was hot and dirty, but this is different. He may not understand why I bought a toy like this.

I know Sean never would've understood. Shortly before we broke up, I tried to express to him once my desire to be bred, even if it was just role play. He laughed at me.

"You're a hot badass bitch, remember, Alex?" I say out loud. I put my stupid ex out of my mind and decide to just go with it. If Elijah chooses to take me up on my offer, would it really be bad if he walked in on me using this? He didn't judge me for anything I said or did last night, which is already more than I can say about most of the men I've been with.

Toy in hand, I take a step toward the bed and stop. The expensive and insanely high thread-count sheets stare at me as if to say: *Don't even think about it, Alex.* If they stain, I'll be headed for an interesting conversation with my parents.

Though if it was Elijah's cum, I'd be more inclined not to care. Arousal floods between my legs at the picture of his release dripping down my thighs while he pants above me, fucking it back inside my tight heat.

Alright. Yep. I need to get off. Turning on my heel, I head toward the bathroom. I set the toy on the Jack-and-Jill sink before opening the glass doors of the way-too-big shower that could comfortably fit five or more people. Then I turn on the rainforest showerhead and adjust the temperature to my liking before I retreat to the sink.

I read the instructions on how to use the toy before I came here. I need to put the lube in the syringe and fill the chamber inside the toy. Then, when I want to release it, I use the remote.

Seems easy enough. I pick up the lube at the same time I catch my reflection in the mirror.

I don't normally sleep naked, but I was hoping Elijah would be in my bed by now and didn't see the point in bothering with clothes. With a sigh, I run my free hand over my light red hair, which is a total mess from all the tossing and turning I did. Then my hand travels down my generously curvy hip to my round stomach before I turn to the side.

Allie has tried to placate me by telling me I have plenty of time to have children, which is true. Lots of women have babies well into their forties. But I always thought I'd be a mom by now, and as I told Elijah, I thought that's what my ex-fiancé wanted, too. In hindsight, that's not a good reason to marry someone. But to be fair, I did love him, and I know he loved me. The relationship was just weird and complicated.

I think we both wanted something from each other, and in the end, we couldn't get it. Now I'm starting over. In Los Angeles. Which is probably one of the worst places to date, to find someone who wants to settle down and have kids.

Steam begins to fog up the mirror, and I decide to lean into my desires, to this side of me that Sean thought was odd. I open the lube cap and fill the syringe then grab the silicone toy. Once it's filled, I step into the shower and place it along with the waterproof controller on the tiled bench inside. When the hot water from the shower hits my back, I sigh. The feeling triggers images of me between Elijah's knees in the hot tub last night.

I trail my hand over my now hard nipples and then down my stomach before reaching the neatly trimmed tuft of ginger curls between my legs. When my fingers touch my clit, I exhale a small whimper and drop my head back until the shower wets my hair. Elijah's sapphire-blue irises appear behind my eyelids, and I imagine his fingers between my legs. I apply more pressure to my sensitive skin and use my other hand to pinch my nipple.

"Elijah," I cry softly, circling my clit as I become wetter. I do that for a minute until my body is strung tight, then I spread my legs a bit to slip a finger inside my entrance. I hum in pleasure, inserting another finger and scissoring them inside me before pulling back out to massage my clit with the wetness.

I'm already so turned on from my thoughts of him while in bed that I decide I'm ready for the toy. I grab it along with the remote and lean on the shower wall so some of the spray still hits me. I want to control the movement, so I hold it instead of suctioning it to the wall, positioning it at my entrance.

I slide the thick head of it in, moaning at the slight burn of it. Using the hand holding the small controller, I pull on my nipple and turn the vibration on. I cry out and push more of the toy in, imagining it's Elijah's cock instead of a fake one, that it's his hands on me instead of my own.

"Fuck!" I feed it in another inch, then another. "Yes, Elijah, please," I beg. My imagination is running wild as I glide my hand up my throat and press my thumb into my racing pulse like he did last night.

I cry out again as the girth of the toy stretches me. I can't help but think what it would feel like to have Elijah's real cock in me. It's similar in girth but longer than this one. I bet I'd feel him all the way in my throat if he thrust into me hard enough.

More arousal floods my pussy as I begin to fuck myself slowly with the toy, my head falling back as the vibrations of it pulse through my body in a teasing pattern. I squeeze my throat harder, careful not to press the button on the remote. I'm saving that for last.

Chest heaving, I imagine Elijah fucking me harder into the wall, his toned ass flexing as he plunges into me in rough strokes. How his cock would look sliding in and out of my entrance, coated in my arousal. I shove the toy into me harder, and my body tightens like a bowstring as my orgasm approaches.

Running my hand back down my body, I rub my clit harder, hearing Elijah's rough voice in my ear praising me, telling me how good I'm taking his cock. How he wants to fill me up, claim me, make me his.

"Yes, Elijah, please. Fill me up." I moan wildly, my head falling back as I stroke myself harder, my eyes watering from how turned on I am.

"Yes!" The wave of tension in my body crests at the same time I register the sound of the shower door opening. I see a flash of silver hair, and then my eyes go wide as Elijah's feral blue gaze meets mine. I don't have time to react before his lips are crushed to mine and I'm being completely devoured.

CHAPTER TEN

Elijah

MY LIPS COLLIDE INTO Alex's as warm water pelts us and steam floats in the air. She gasps into my mouth, her body still shaking from her orgasm as the toy she was using and something else clatters to the ground.

"Elijah," she murmurs against my lips.

"You started without me," I grumble, kicking the objects at my feet away and spinning her so that her breasts press against the tiles. Her breath hitches in her throat at the sudden movement.

"I didn't think you were coming," she says quietly.

"Put your hands above your head with your palms pressed against the wall." A sound of surprise mixed with arousal escapes her lips, but she does as I ask. "Now arch your ass back."

"Elijah," she moans, a curious lilt to her voice.

I gently slap the wet skin of her butt, the ivory turning pink at the light smack. She cries out but pushes her ass back, and delight fills my stomach that she liked it.

I bring my hand down again on the other cheek, the action echoing in the shower. "You've been a dirty girl without me, Alex."

Her head turns so she can look over her shoulder, and a little smirk appears on her lips. "Then punish me for it."

My already throbbing cock aches. While my desire to pull her out of this shower and put her over my knee is strong, I have other ideas. Ideas that can't wait.

"Keep your hands on the wall," I command, moving behind her and grabbing her hips. I pull her back into my groin so she can feel what she's done to me, how hard I am for her after watching the little show she put on.

She moans as my cock slides between her ass cheeks, my hips gently thrusting as I dig my blunt nails into her hips. "Imagine my surprise," I say, leaning into her body so my lips tease against her ear, "when I got to your bedroom and saw the door cracked open for me, only to find the bed empty." I bite down on her earlobe, and she arches her sweet ass further into me.

"I didn't think you were coming," she reiterates. I pull back to smack her skin, and she moans again.

"You know what I think, Alex?" I ask rhetorically. "I think you were too turned on to wait. That you're an impatient girl."

She bites her lower lip as I grip her hips harder, pulling her delicious ass into me and grinding on her.

"Are you, Alex? Are you an impatient girl, needy for my cock?"

She nods, her hands clawing at the tile like she is trying desperately not to touch me. I smirk and nip at her ear again. "Say it. Tell me what you are."

"I'm an impatient girl, needy for your cock."

"Yes, you are," I hum as my hand winds around the curve of her waist to find the V between her legs. I thumb her swollen clit, and she keens. "Sensitive?"

She nods. "Yes."

My eyes dart to the floor to see the silicone dildo still vibrating on the ground, and a stupid rage fills me. I have nothing against toys, but I do have something against not being the one to use them on her. It's idiotic, but I can't help it. While I'm with this woman, I want to give her every pleasure. By *my* hand. By *my* mouth. By *my* cock.

Alex presses her pleading body into me, and I nip at the wet skin of her shoulder, pinching her clit so she sucks in a breath. "From now on, you don't use toys unless I'm in the room.

Unless I'm the one to fuck you with them or I tell you how to fuck yourself, understood?"

Alex glances back at me, her pupils dark and cheeks red like cherries. "You're accepting my offer?"

My face softens, the fact that she's wanting reassurance even though I'm already here tugging on my heart. "One weekend." I rub her clit in slow, lazy circles. "You have me."

Her eyes shine, and any doubts I still had leave my mind. One weekend. I'm giving myself one weekend to live in sin with this incredibly beautiful woman.

I'll beat myself up about it later, but I know I won't regret it. There's no way I would be able to. I'll worry about how I'm going to look my best friend in the eye when I get home, but that's not important now. In fact, with his daughter rubbing her ass against my cock and her slippery arousal on my fingers, I doubt anything will be as important as the time I spend with Alex.

"Then what are you waiting for, Mr. Serious?" she challenges.

I relax my brow with a smile and take my cock in my hand, gathering some of her wetness so it slips easily up and down the crease of her ass. On the third pass, I push the swollen head against her tight ring of muscles.

She gasps. "Elijah!"

I press in a tiny bit but don't force anything. I know better than that. "Has anyone ever taken your ass, Alex?"

She leans her forehead against the shower wall at the subtle pressure. "No, never."

I dip the tip of my cock in enough that she whines before pulling back. "I'm going to take this tight hole of yours, Alex. Not right now, but before we leave this house, it's mine. Will you let me?" I repeat the action again, slipping it in enough to make her react.

"Yes!" she cries. "Please, Elijah. I'll let you do anything you want to me. Just take me now. Please. I need to feel you."

Her pleading ignites a desire to claim her deep within me. To show her that no fake dick is going to satisfy her. Only I can.

I mold myself to her back, bringing her hands down from the wall. When they're at her sides, I spin her to face me. We're both soaked from the shower now, our chests heaving in anticipation.

I brush her darkened red hair from her face, claiming her lips with mine. Her hands claw at my back as she hitches her leg over my hip, grinding herself on me. We moan into each other's mouths while I taste her again and again, her hard nipples dragging across my chest. I break the kiss and lap the water off her sweet skin, sucking on her clavicle as my cock throbs against the perfect curves of her soft stomach.

"Elijah." My name falls from her lips like a prayer. I place my hands on the underside of her ribs, brushing my thumbs over her nipples. Her head lands back against the tile, and her chest thrusts out like an offering. I latch my lips onto the hardened buds and suck, squeezing her heavy breasts until she's practically sobbing with need.

"I love your body, Alex," I say between bites and sucks. "You're all mine, aren't you?"

"I'm yours."

"You want my cock, you dirty girl?" I work my way back up her chest and neck to kiss her lips. Once. Twice. Then a third time.

"Yes, Elijah!" She pouts so prettily. "No more teasing."

I meet her desire-filled eyes as I fist my cock, circling it around her clit so my pre-cum massages into her sensitive skin. She arches into the sensation, hitching her leg further up my hip so I'm positioned at her entrance.

"Are you on the pill?" I ask, hoping she is because I didn't bring any condoms on this trip. I didn't even think to bring them since I was supposed to be here alone.

She bites her lower lip. "I have an IUD."

I notch my cock inside her tight pussy, the pulsing heat of it making me pause. The gravity of what I'm about to do settles inside me. I'm about to fuck Alex Martin bare. In my best friend's house. In his fucking shower.

It should disgust me, but it only makes me want to give in even more. To sink into her pink cunt and forget about reality. To make our own reality here, together. Even if it's only for a weekend.

"Fill me up, Elijah," she begs, her voice barely a whisper.

A growl leaves my lips at her words, the words I also heard her say while getting herself off to mental images of me. With one swift thrust, I sheath myself inside her, the sound of our bodies meeting as I bottom out echoing through the room. We both curse in pleasure, my forehead resting on Alex's as we feel our bodies intimately connected for the first time, with nothing between us.

Her fingernails dig into my shoulder blades, and I take in a choppy breath. It's been two years since I've had sex with anyone. Two years of being sex-deprived, intimacy-deprived, and simply deprived of human connection beyond work and time with friends. My body shivers, completely unexpected emotion clogging my throat.

I pull back slightly to take in Alex's face, her forehead pinched in pleasure and pupils dilated. She's so incredibly sexy like this. I kiss a diamond pattern of freckles on her cheek then trail my mouth down her neck, licking the water droplets from her flushed skin.

"Elijah," she whimpers. "You feel so good inside me."

Her praise has my spine tingling, and I know I need to move. I pull back and start punching my hips in measured, shallow thrusts. Alex's mouth drops open in an O shape as she clenches her already tight inner walls around me.

"*Fuuuck,*" I exhale. "Keep that up, dirty girl, and this will be over soon."

"I don't care; I need you now."

I click my tongue against the back of my teeth. "So impatient."

Alex slinks her hands down my shoulders to palm my ass. She digs her nails into my flesh hard enough that I know they'll leave perfect crescent-shaped marks.

"Are you claiming me?" I muse as I thrust into her again, a little harder this time.

She groans, nodding a heated *yes* as her nails dig deeper. "Please! I need you, baby. Make me feel you for days."

Between her plea and term of endearment—along with another purposeful squeeze of her cunt—I lose my barely there composure. I pull my cock nearly all the way out then slam back into her heat, my hand slapping against the wall beside her head.

Alex jumps, her sound of surprise turning into a cry that I swallow with my mouth. I become ravenous as I pump into her again and again, a man with everything and nothing to lose all at the same time.

She flexes her hands on my ass, pulling me closer so that my thrusts go deeper. I curse at the feeling, at my balls slapping against her skin and the noise her wet pussy is making from our coupling. It's heavenly, better than the best music in the world, and it only spurs me to thrust harder, deeper.

"Fuck!" she cries when I hit her G-spot, her eyes rolling back into her head.

"You like that, Alex?" I bring my other hand up to grasp her throat like I saw her do to herself before I interrupted.

"Yes! God, yes!" she chants in time with my hips.

Her greedy pussy starts to flutter, and I know she's close to coming. "Look at me," I grunt as I continue to thrust.

Her eyes open to find mine, filled with lust and excitement. My stare matches hers as I add gentle pressure to her throat, taking my other hand off the wall so I can rub her clit. She sighs at the contact, her body seeking more as I bring her toward the brink.

"You're going to come on my cock, Alex. And you're going to take everything I give you, understand?" She nods vigorously, biting her bottom lip. I restrict her air a bit more, watching her carefully for any signs of distress as I fuck her recklessly now. She whines out my name in a breathless moan as the sounds of us together get louder, and my balls tighten, signaling I'm close to the end.

I lick into her mouth, squeezing her throat and taking her whimpers into me as she starts to crest. When her pussy clenches and her body stills, I trap her lower lip between mine and bite down until she cries out.

"That's it," I croon, memorizing the way she looks right now, burning it into my brain so I never forget this moment. Then I release her throat and thread my fingers in her hair.

"Elijah." She trembles. "Come inside me. I need it. *Please*, I need it!"

Her words combined with the heaven of her cunt around me pushes me over the edge, and I give her what she needs. My cum unloads into her, spilling inside her rope after rope as I continue to fuck her in short, forceful thrusts.

"*Yes!*" She practically weeps, her body clinging to mine as she comes yet again with my thumb pressed to her clit. Her pussy milks me for every drop of my cum as my head falls against her shoulder in satisfaction. My hips slow as my orgasm fires through my body.

We stand there for a while, crushed together as the water sprays around us. When I finally look into her sated eyes, I see they're glassy with tears. Panic wells in my stomach, and I try to pull back, but she stops me. Her hands hold me tight so we remain connected.

"Did I hurt you?" I ask.

She shakes her head. "No, the opposite." She brushes some wet hair from my forehead and runs a thumb over my brow. "It was just intense. My body's way of coming down."

I exhale my relief, pressing my lips to hers in a slow, lazy kiss. When I pull back, she's smiling gently, and her breathing has calmed.

"I'm going to pull out now, alright?" She nods, her gaze dropping down to where we're still joined as I start to remove myself, my softening cock slipping from her body. When my release drips from her sex, coating her wet thighs before dropping to the tile to be washed away, I have the intense desire to push it back in.

I don't have time to analyze that thought, though, because Alex's hand trails down her flushed body before she swipes a finger through the mess. With a sultry glint in her eye, she opens her mouth and places the digit on her tongue. Then seductively sucks it clean.

Goddamn. I'm in so much trouble with this woman.

CHAPTER ELEVEN

Alex

ELIJAH ISN'T LIKE ANY man I've met. After we had sex, I expected him to be like my other partners and quickly clean then leave the shower. But I should've known he'd be different, especially after we had such intense sex together. More intense than I ever thought possible. Sex that embarrassingly made me tear up at the end.

Once we'd both come down from our orgasms, he'd taken his time washing me, massaging my scalp with shampoo before conditioning it. He even let it sit while he gently washed every nook and cranny of my body in meticulous strokes, taking time to clean away the evidence of his release between my legs. Even if I secretly didn't want him to.

I flush. He hasn't said anything about the toy I used. After we finished showering, he'd picked it up off the ground but didn't say a word. I didn't miss the genuine curiosity on his face as he cleaned it like he washed my body, with care and attention. I know I'll have to explain it to him eventually. Or maybe I won't. But it was awkward for me, nonetheless.

I lay back naked against the pillows of the bed and take a slow breath, my thoughts turning nicer as Elijah walks out of the bathroom in all his naked glory. My eyes find the gift between his legs, and a smile tugs at the corner of my lips. My sore inner walls clench at the memory of it moving within me.

Immediately, I want him inside me again, to feel that fullness I've never felt before today. But I'm trying to be patient. Even if watching him dry off his lean body isn't helping to calm my raging desire for him again.

He makes eye contact with me as he runs the towel over his short silver hair. The backdrop of the lake behind him and his relaxed features pull at my chest. It's really nice to see this version of him, the carefree one that's been hiding under Mr. Serious.

He folds his towel neatly then puts it over the back of a chair before joining me on the bed. For a brief moment, I wonder how I should react. Is this going to be the type of arrangement where we act cordial after we fuck? Or is he a cuddler?

I don't have to wonder long, because as soon as he's settled on the bed, he pulls my body into his. Warmth and contentment fill me as I lay my head on his chest, his arms wrapping around me in a safe cocoon.

"How are you feeling?" he asks.

I hum as I run my fingers through his chest hair. "Like I just had the best sex of my life."

"Really?" he asks, genuine surprise in his tone.

I shift and tilt my chin up to look at his face, his warm palm now resting in the dip of my waist. The little furrow has returned to his brow, and I laugh softly. "Yes, really. You know how to use this body of yours. And this," I say, gently cupping his cock. "You *really* know how to use this."

Elijah's eyes darken, and he reaches down to grab my hand. I pout playfully as he moves it away, but I like the fact he's now holding my hand, so I don't pout long.

He laces our fingers together and places them on his hip. "I need a little time to recover."

I eye his already half-hard erection. "You look fine to me."

He shakes his head and lifts the hand he's holding to kiss my knuckles. "Later, my dirty impatient girl." He half grins.

Between the sweet action and the new nicknames, my thighs squeeze together, and I have to try very hard to keep myself from pouncing on him again, from being exactly what he called me. So I decide I need to change the subject.

"I'm glad you decided to stay."

He rubs his hand down my back. "Me, too."

I lift my head so I can see him again. His eyes are closed now, his body at ease as he strokes my skin and smiles at whatever he's thinking. "What made you take my offer?"

Elijah opens his eyes, his hand squeezing mine. "Because I wanted to."

"That's all?"

He sits up against the pillows, tugging me with him. "What other reason would I need?"

I shrug. "To taste the forbidden fruit."

His hand on my back stills, and I regret what I said. I didn't mean it as more than teasing. But I think a part of me is curious, especially given he wasn't sure he should stay last night. He was so dead set on leaving from the beginning.

"Alex," he says quietly. "Please don't think this was some challenge for me. I'll admit, there's an exciting element to us being together. But I didn't stay for the risk."

I raise my eyebrow at him and hold his hand tighter. "For the reward, then?" My tone is unserious as I try to convey to him that I'm not upset, no matter the reason he stayed. Because I wanted the reward, too. I wanted the release, too. That's how this all started, anyway.

He shoots me a playful yet chiding look. "As I said, I stayed because I wanted to. If it wasn't clear at dinner last night or in the hot tub or the shower..." He smiles now. "I like you, Alex. I want to spend the weekend with you. Even if we don't have sex again, I'd stay to get to know you better, to spend the time relaxing with you. The only reason I didn't come seek you out earlier this morning is because I wanted to let you rest. Not because I didn't want you."

My cheeks tinge pink at his sincerity and the fact that I had doubts he wasn't going to take me up on my offer. Though if he hadn't, I would've understood.

"To be clear, I want that, too, to get to know you better." I brush my hand up his chest, his muscles trembling under my touch. "But, we'll definitely be having sex again."

"Oh, yeah?" he asks, a lift in his voice.

I prop myself up enough that my bare breasts brush against him. "So much sex." I skim my lips over his. "I also seem to remember something about you taking my ass for the first time?"

His gaze intensifies, blue eyes dilating as his hand trails down my back, stopping at the swell of my butt. "I'd really be your first?" he asks.

"You would."

"Hmm, such a sweet thing to give me. Are you sure?"

"More than sure," I say, already getting wet at the prospect of him taking me there, of experiencing something totally new with him.

His hand slips further down and squeezes one of my cheeks. "Do you have a butt plug?"

My eyes widen. "You know what a butt plug is?"

He barks a laugh. "I'm not that ancient, Alex. Nor a prude, like some may believe."

I shake my head, "I didn't mean—"

He cuts me off with a kiss. "I'm just teasing you. But yes, I know what a butt plug is. Do you have one?" He eyes my suitcase on the floor.

"No, I don't."

"Hmm, well, I'll improvise," he says, running a finger down the crease of my ass. "Maybe we can use that fake cock of yours."

My nostrils flare. "That's almost as big as yours!" The shine in his eye tells me that he's joking. I tug on his well-trimmed salt-and-pepper beard and push out my bottom lip. "You're right. You can be very unserious, Mr. Serious."

He rumbles with laughter. "Speaking of toys—and you don't have to answer this, so please tell me if it makes you uncomfortable."

I try to stay relaxed, knowing what's coming. I do feel like I owe him an explanation, even if I really don't. I exhale. "You can ask me anything."

He brushes the pad of his thumb over the apple of my cheek. "That toy, it had lube in it, right?"

I flush. "Yes, it did."

He continues to brush his thumb over my cheek. "Don't be embarrassed. I shouldn't have said anything."

"No, no. It's okay. Please, ask me."

His hand on my ass grips me tighter, pulling me closer to him. "What's the purpose of it?"

I play with the hairs of his beard, focusing on the way the colors mix together. "Um, well, the reason I said I wanted you to fill me up..." I flush harder. "I like the way it feels when..."

"...when a man comes inside you?" he finishes for me.

"Yes," I breathe out. "The thought of being filled, of being bred. It turns me on."

Elijah lifts my chin. His eyes are even darker now, and I don't miss the way his cock twitches. "Bred?"

I nod. "Getting pregnant. The idea of it. It—gosh, this is so embarrassing."

"Like I said, you have no reason to be embarrassed. It's incredibly sexy, Alex."

"Really?"

His gaze darts to his erection, a half smile on his lips. "I think I'm turned on by that as well, it would seem. I liked seeing my cum dripping out of you. It was..."

"...hot?" I finish for him this time.

"More than hot. Beautiful. Sensual."

"I know I don't have to say this, but I want you to know since we're having unprotected sex: This doesn't mean I want you to get me pregnant. I wasn't lying when I said I have an IUD. I can show you my records online if you want."

His mouth drops open, and his features turn hard with anger. "Why in the world would I ever think that or ask that of you?"

My stomach flips, and I shrug. "When I expressed to my ex what I liked, he said it was because I was so desperate for babies. He was worried I would do something rash, and he wasn't ready for children. I tried to explain to him that while I wanted to start a family, it's a kink. A pretty popular one."

Elijah's brow pinches, and his eyes narrow. "Your ex is an asshole. Oliver was right for not liking him. I would never think so terribly of you, Alex. Never. But with that said, I know the risks of unprotected sex. But I trust you. I've known your dad for a long time now—" He stops himself, realizing he brought up my dad and sex in practically the same sentence.

I smile weakly. "Thank you. That means a lot to me. And I'm sorry if this is weird for you."

He shakes his head. "I'm fine, Alex. Thank you for sharing that with me. You don't have to be embarrassed to say or do anything around me. You're an adult. You aren't hurting anyone. And like I said, I want to be here. I'm choosing to be here. Like you are."

I kiss his chest and exhale a quiet sigh of relief. "Thank you."

He brushes his fingers up my side. "No thanks needed."

We lay there for a while, his touch easing my mind as I wonder if somehow the universe brought Elijah to me, a man who doesn't judge me. Who wants to have no-strings-attached fun. Who even seems to like what I like.

It's almost too perfect, like a complete and utter dream. I smile, thinking about how Allie is going to lose her mind when I share what happened this weekend.

"Tell me something about yourself," I say, propping myself up so I can see him better.

"Anything in particular?"

I run the pad of my pointer finger over his nipple, watching it come alive under my touch. "What do you like to do for fun?

He tucks a half-dry piece of hair behind my ear. "To be honest, I haven't done much on the side of fun in recent years."

"Why is that?"

"Without going into it too much, I went through a divorce last year that was messy. After that, I threw myself into work. I golf with the guys here and there, but mostly, my days are pretty much the same."

I frown. "I'm sorry to hear that."

He traces my lower lip with his thumb. "Don't be. Much like your situation, Deb and I weren't compatible. I only wish we would've figured it out earlier."

I kiss the pad of his thumb. "How long were you married?"

"Ten years." My mouth drops open, and he chuckles. "Please don't feel sorry for me. It was good at first, and I don't have regrets. But we didn't have children, and she developed new interests and started her own business. We naturally drifted apart. It happens."

"But the divorce was messy?" I ask curiously.

"We co-owned a lot of assets together, and she got a little petty, though I think it was her way to try to save the marriage. But in the end, I knew it was time for us both to move on. I wanted to see who or what else life had to offer me."

I sit up on the bed, Elijah's eyes drifting down toward my still-naked breasts. When his eyes meet mine, he's smiling like a dog. I smack his arm. "Besides my amazing breasts."

He huffs a laugh. "They are amazing."

"Be serious!"

He sits up off the pillows and reaches out to fondle one. My breath catches in my throat as he does it. But then as quickly as his touch is there, it's gone, leaving me wanting more.

"I was being serious," he teases. "But if you really want to know what I had in mind, it's another similarity to you."

My eyebrows shoot up. "Really? You want to enter your hot-girl badass-bitch era, too?" He looks at me funny, and I snort. "It's nothing. I'll tell you later. Go on."

"Well, just so I don't forget to say it, you're already both of those things—minus the bitch part. At least from what I see and what you told me." He tugs me into him so our backs are now both up against the wall of pillows. "And if I understand what you mean, I think I had one of those phases in college."

That makes me blush and laugh all at the same time. "You were a ladies' man, weren't you?"

He develops a look that says I'm right. It isn't hard to picture since Elijah is so insanely gorgeous now—I can only imagine a younger version of him surrounded by college girls. I bet he was beating them off with a stick.

"But to answer your question..." He pauses for a moment, his brow settling into his default pinch. "I've always wanted to have a family. Kids. Maybe even a dog. A legacy to leave behind."

My heart thuds in my chest at his words, and I swear a spark lights in my stomach. One that feels an awful lot like...hope. I try to swallow the feeling and keep any sign of my thoughts off my face. The last thing I want to do is scare this man off after I said we were going to have a weekend of no-strings-attached fun.

Catching feelings and thinking about marriage and babies is not no strings attached. Those are in fact, a lot of strings. And none of those strings can happen between us. At least not in Elijah's mind. If I'm being realistic, I know they shouldn't happen, either. If Elijah and I were together in real life, we'd run into a lot of complications. The biggest one being my dad.

"The good news is, you can still find someone to have that with," I say, even though my stomach sours when I speak the words. "And you should get a dog."

Elijah stares at me thoughtfully. I have no idea what he's thinking, but I like the way he's looking at me, like maybe he's having the same thoughts. That maybe he's picturing me pregnant with his child, a German shepherd named Dolly at my feet.

I force a small smile and try to pretend I'm not acting like the teenage version of myself that used to write Mrs. insert-the-last-name-of-the-cute-boy-I-just-met-here all over my notebook.

"Do you like dogs?" he asks.

I clear my throat. "Yes. I love dogs. German shepherds are my favorite."

His eyes widen. "You're joking?"

"Don't tell me that's your favorite breed?"

He nods. "I had one when I was a child," he says almost sadly. But then he's smiling again. "His name was Fred."

I huff a laugh. "Fred?"

"I liked the Flintstones."

My belly warms thinking of Elijah as a little boy watching his favorite cartoon with his dog. Then my unhinged brain starts to wonder what our kids would look like, what our life would be on a weekend morning together. I would cook him and the kids breakfast before we took Dolly—or Fred—for a walk in the park. I'd grade papers on a Sunday night while he caught up on work or helped the kids with their homework.

His thumb on my cheek brings me back to reality, a reality where that isn't possible. *Or is it?* An interesting idea pops into my mind and begins to run wild.

"What are you thinking about, Alex?" Elijah asks curiously.

I stare into his blue eyes. They're so sweet, so caring. I've never had a man look at me like this before. Like I'm...treasured.

"It's silly," I say, though the words are on the tip of my tongue.

Elijah traces a cluster of freckles on my cheek. The motion causes a tickling sensation in my gut. "Nothing you could say would be silly to me, Alex." He brushes his knuckle over my cheekbone and down the round curve of my shoulder, stopping only when he gets to my hand. Then he links them together and squeezes. "But only tell me if you want to."

He doesn't break eye contact with me, and I believe every word he says. He didn't judge me for my toys or my kink. He didn't judge me about Sean or anything I've told me so far. I decide I should just say what I'm thinking. If he truly thinks I'm banana bonkers, I'll leave and go back to LA. No hard feelings.

"I, um…" I try to collect my thoughts, mulling on the best way to say this. "I was thinking that since we both want the same things that, um…maybe you'd want to play house with me this weekend?"

I think Elijah stops breathing when I finish my ask. The words I allowed to come out of my mouth seem to echo in the room. Gosh, why did I say that out loud? Who asks someone that? Apparently me.

"You know what?" I retract my hand from his. "Forget I said anything. That *was* silly, and I shouldn't have said it. I'll get dressed and let you do what you want to do for the day." My movement on the bed snaps him out of his trance, and before I can get away from him, I'm being pinned to the bed by a very naked Elijah. A very naked and *aroused* Elijah.

His hard length presses into the fat of my belly, and I bite my lip as I gaze into his heated blue eyes. "You want to pretend to be my wife?"

The wetness from my mouth goes straight to my vagina at his words. *My wife.* Holy hell, I love the sound of that. I lick my lips and nod slowly. "We could pretend we were married, do a little role play, and see how it feels." His cock twitches against my belly, and I smile. "I know you've been married before, but it sounds like it wasn't how you pictured it?"

He shakes his head.

"I want to give you what you want, Elijah," I almost whisper. "Will you let me?"

His lips are closer to mine now, his grip on my wrists he's got pinned at my sides tightening. "You've already given me what I want, Alex. I want to give you everything *you* want."

My gaze softens. How is this man even real? "Trust me. You'll be giving me what I want," I assure him. But what I really want to say is: *You'll be giving me a fantasy I've always wanted to live out, Elijah. Having a man who cares for me, who adores and appreciates me, who likes the food I cook and doesn't judge me. Who lets me be a badass independent woman but also lets me serve and appreciate him. And he does the same for me in return.* But of course, I don't. Instead, I try to convey it all through my gaze.

Elijah releases one of my wrists and brushes his pointer finger down the side of my face adoringly before grasping my chin. "You're an amazing woman, Alex."

I flush from his attention. "I'm honestly surprised you're not running away. I know it's a weird idea."

He shakes his head. "Don't put yourself down for voicing what you want. You're brave; I admire that."

I think I turn redder. "You really don't think it's weird?"

Elijah's gaze intensifies as he increases the pressure of his cock on my belly, a bit of pre-cum wetting my skin. A small moan leaves my lips, and he nips at my mouth with his.

"Does it seem like I think it's weird?"

"Is that a yes, then?"

He kisses up my chin as he grinds against me. When he traces the shell of my ear with his nose, my breath hitches in my throat.

"It's a yes...*wife*."

Then his lips are on mine in a consuming kiss, and his cock is sheathed deep inside me.

Chapter Twelve

Elijah

If this is a dream, I don't want to wake up from it.

Alex's gentle humming fills my ears as I sip the orange juice she poured me from my seat at the kitchen island. I can't keep my eyes off her as she floats around the kitchen packing up a picnic basket for a beach day, the blue floral-patterned sundress she asked me to pick out for her twirling around her thighs.

I bite my cheek and think how ridiculous it is that I agreed to a beach day—I hate the sand. And lakes aren't exactly my favorite thing to swim in, though Alex insists that we'll be able to see the bottom. But her smile was so bright when she suggested the activity, I couldn't say no. There was also a promise of a string bikini if I came with her. And isn't compromise what marriage is all about?

Marriage. I've never role played before, but when Alex suggested it, I couldn't help the excitement I felt, how fucking hard I got at the idea of calling her mine—even if it's fake. It might be something some people would say I need my head checked for, but I strongly disagree. I may be older, but I'm an open-minded man. Before my marriage with Deb turned monotonous, we were sexually adventurous in our own way. Not like Alex is, but I'm not completely vanilla, either.

I'm more dominant and always have been in the bedroom. Dirty talk is something I enjoy, and it's been incredibly freeing to let that part of myself come out after it being dormant for so long. I may have also searched the internet for what Alex liked while she got ready.

A breeding kink.

My cock hardens in my shorts, and I let my eyes drift to the space between her legs as she wraps the sandwiches she's made in parchment paper as if she stepped out of a homemaker magazine.

The idea of my cum still inside her as she works, the fantasy that she could be pregnant with my child is...sexy, to say the least. During my search, I also did a deep dive into a couple of online forums to see how I could make this little role play of ours even more exciting for her. I hope I have the balls to do it when we're intimate again. And boy, do I plan on being very intimate with her, as many times as she'll allow me to before the end of tomorrow.

My gut twists at the thought of leaving, but I quickly shake it away. I have limited time with Alex, so I'm going to make the most of it.

"What kind of chips do you like?" she asks as she makes her way to the pantry.

My eyes drift to her ass, and I picture how it looks under her dress. The string bikini I know she has on underneath leaves little to the imagination, just like her thong did yesterday.

She turns her head over her shoulder when I don't answer and shoots me a knowing look. *Busted.* I smile lopsidedly. "Any kind. You pick."

She grabs a bag and holds it up. "Can't go wrong with plain kettle chips." Then she walks back over and places them in the basket. When she's satisfied we have everything we need, she closes the wicker top. "Ready to go get our beach on?"

I chuckle. "If we must."

Her lip curls, and she moves to stand behind me, looping her arms around my waist. When her lips kiss my shoulder, I lean back into her, absorbing her warmth and soaking in her presence.

"If you don't want to go, we don't have to. Or I can go myself and meet you back here later. I don't mind."

I grab her arm and shift us so we're facing each other, our bodies pressed together with her arms locked behind my neck. "What kind of husband would I be if I didn't go with my wife to the beach?"

A lovely pink flush appears between the valley of her breasts then crawls up her neck till her freckled cheeks are pink.

"I'm going with you, Alex. Plus, if I don't go, who will rub you down with sunscreen?" I waggle my eyebrows. Her sexy laugh floats around us, and I pull her close, our noses bumping. "I'll be fine at the beach for a couple of hours. Especially since I'll be with you."

Alex's eyes soften, and she pecks me on the lips. When she goes to pull away, I tug her back, kissing her longer. When my hand starts to find its way up her dress, she darts out of my arms before I can catch her.

"If we don't leave now, we'll miss the warmest part of the day."

I want to say that I'll keep her warm. Instead, I stand, grabbing my messenger bag at my feet along with the beach bag she filled with towels and sunscreen—plus a little something special I slipped in.

Alex looks at my messenger bag and lifts an eyebrow in question. "I said bring a book or something, not your work bag."

I bite the inside of my cheek. She sounded so much like Oliver for a second. "It's not work." She crosses her arms over her ample chest, and I chuckle at how serious she looks. "It's not, I promise. It *is* my computer, but I'm bringing it in case I'm inspired to write."

The hard line of her lips softens, and then her green eyes shine. "You're a writer?"

I shake my head. "I wouldn't say that. I write copy for work, but I've always wanted to write a book. Another thing I thought I'd try in this new phase of my life."

"What kind of books do you want to write?"

"Thrillers."

She pulls the picnic basket off the counter, her smile as bright as the sun. "You know, I can see that."

Alex starts to walk toward the back door, and I follow dutifully. "Really?"

She studies my face as I pull the beach bag up on my shoulder so I can open the sliding door for her. "You're an intellectual, seeking adventure in your life, and you're curious. I can totally see it."

Her analysis of my personality stuns me for a second. "I suppose you've hit the nail on the head."

She smiles, and I place a hand on the small of her back as we walk into the nice, sunny day. "I won't lie, I'm not really a thriller person, but I would read the shit out of your book."

"Because you're my wife?" I tease.

Her smile shines brighter as she grabs my free hand and kisses my cheek. "Even if I wasn't"—she gives me a playful wink—"I would because I want to. Because you wrote it."

I squeeze her hand, that feeling of contentedness settling in my bones as we continue to walk down several flights of wooden stairs to a private beach and a long dock that leads out onto the water. When we get to the bottom, Alex lets go of my hand and removes her sandals, stepping onto the beach with a sigh.

She wiggles her toes in the sand. "Are you coming?"

I take off my own sandals and pick them up before venturing onto the sand. The heat of it burns the bottoms of my feet, but I smile anyway. Alex presses her lips together as she watches me, trying not to laugh.

"You really hate the beach, don't you?"

I grimace, not wanting her to feel bad that I came down here with her. I really do want to spend time with her. "It's not that

I hate it. I love going to the ocean. But I view it from a nice waterfront restaurant or a patio. Sand gets everywhere. And the ocean has sharks."

A belly laugh bubbles up and out of her. "Good thing this is a lake, then. And like I said before, you can see the bottom. No big fish will try to eat you here."

"Thank god," I say playfully, willing to make fun of myself though my reasons for hating the beach are legitimate and valid.

With another small chuckle under her breath, she starts to walk again, motioning for me to follow her until we reach a spot near the water's edge.

"Here okay?" she asks. I nod, wanting to say I don't care where we sit as long as I'm sitting next to her. But that's an obvious statement considering it's just the two of us on a private beach that's blocked off by the trees and a rocky landscape on either side.

"Is this a manmade beach?" I ask as we start to spread out a large beach towel and pull things from our bags.

"I think it's naturally a pretty rocky beach. But Dad has sand brought in year-round so we can enjoy it instead of always having to sunbathe on the dock," she says, pulling her dress up and over her head with no warning.

My mouth waters as I take in the vision that is Alex Martin in a green string bikini. Her curvy, dimpled body is nearly naked as she folds her dress and bends to put it in the bag we brought, then she stands to fix the half ponytail she's put her fiery hair in and adjusts the small squares of fabric that are hardly covering her breasts. Or should I say that are hardly covering her nipples.

"Please tell me," I say as I pull my own shirt over my head, "that you've never worn this suit in front of another man before."

Alex takes a step toward me and grabs my shirt from my hands. She folds it exactly how I would've before placing it in the bag alongside her dress.

"Of course not, baby. I bought this for you," she says, a grin tugging at her pink-painted lips.

Now, logically I know she didn't buy the suit for me. But her words hit me in the gut nonetheless. The idea that, if Alex and I were together, she would have bought something like this with me in mind makes me not only very happy but hard as a rock.

Her eyes shift to the now clear bulge in my swim trunks before they trail up and down my body.

"Need help with your...sunscreen?" she asks.

I release a breathy laugh. "I would love that."

She grabs the SPF fifty she told me she has to have or she'll burn and squirts some of it in her hand, motioning for me to turn around. I do as she asks, and she steps behind me.

"This may be a little cold," she warns before she places her hands on my shoulders. I shiver at the cool lotion touching my skin but quickly warm up as Alex's hands travel down my body. I don't miss the way she pays special attention to the muscles of my back and the slopes of my shoulders.

"Has anyone ever called you a silver fox before?" she asks, her voice a tad deeper than usual.

"Not to my face," I say honestly, though I have heard myself called that before, most recently at a hotel in New York when I was on business.

Alex squirts more lotion into her hands, her slippery fingers trailing lower and lower until she's thumbing the elastic of my trunks. I suck in a breath as her hands easily dip inside, cupping my ass and squeezing. My cock that won't stop being hard around her gets harder.

"I don't think the sun reaches inside my shorts," I tease.

"Oh, so you want me to stop?" she asks, her lips near my ear as she presses her breasts into my back.

"I didn't say that."

She hums as she massages the muscles of my glutes, and a small groan leaves my parted lips when she starts to slide her hands around my hips.

Alex places her chin on my shoulder and nibbles at my ear. "How do you feel about a little public indecency?"

I groan as her soft hand grips my erection, and my head turns to meet hers. While I know the beach is private, that doesn't mean we don't run the risk of being seen. The idea of a boater looking on to find me fucking Alex into the sand ignites a primal need to claim her, to show the world who she belongs to. I inhale, trying to calm myself so I don't turn into a barbarian.

"I like a little risk," I manage to say.

With a satisfied noise, Alex presses a short kiss to my lips and pumps my cock through my shorts.

"You know," she says, fisting me harder. "I planned to spend a few hours out here before I had you again." She runs her thumb over the head of my erection, and I hiss. "But I need you inside me, Elijah. I feel empty without your cum filling me up."

Her dirty words hit me hard, and if I hadn't come already this morning, I would've shot my load into my shorts. I grab Alex's wrist to stop her motions. Her eyes grow wide as I pull her hand out from under the elastic and tug her to me so we're facing each other.

I look down at her thumb, glistening with my pre-cum, and I do something I know she'll enjoy. "Open your mouth, and stick your tongue out," I command her.

Her eyes widen, but she does it, her pink tongue darting out. "Suck my cum from your finger, Alex. Show me you won't waste a single drop."

She shifts, her thighs rubbing together. I release her wrist, and she doesn't hesitate to lick the white drop from her finger. A moan reverberates through her as she sucks it off.

"Now, lay on the towel face down, my dirty wife. I've got a surprise for you."

CHAPTER THIRTEEN

Alex

THE HOT SUN BEATS on my back and thighs as I lay on the oversized beach towel. I'm so turned on, I can't think straight. When Elijah calls me his wife, I think my insides melt and my vagina combusts.

Is it possible to get pregnant from words alone? If it were, I'd be pregnant with twins. Or triplets!

I turn my head and rest it on my arm to look up at him. He's holding the sunscreen bottle and sporting the erection I gave him underneath his trunks. I lick my lips, still tasting the saltiness of his cum on my tongue. This man...

Just when I think he can't surprise me more, he surprises me again. He's leaned into this role-play thing like he does it all the time. It honestly threw me at first, but I like it. I probably like it too much.

Elijah gets down on the towel and, without hesitation, straddles me so I can feel his cock prodding my ass, pushing the string of my bikini further between my cheeks in a way that has me squirming. When the cool lotion hits my skin and the smell of coconut fills my nose, I let out a quiet moan.

"I have to say, getting rubbed down with sunscreen isn't the surprise I expected."

Elijah's palms start to rub the lotion into my shoulders, and I can't deny it does feel good. Even if it's not his cock inside me.

"No?" he smirks, massaging his hands lower till he reaches my love handles. Then he stops his descent, moving his hands back up.

"Elijah," I practically whine.

"So impatient for my cock," he tuts, rocking said cock into me like the tease he is.

I groan, but he doesn't stop the task he's set out to do. Instead, he continues to rub every part of me he has access to with sunscreen, working my tense muscles as he goes. By the time he's finished, there's no way I'm getting sunburned. I'm also a puddle of relaxed goo.

Drowsy and incredibly turned on, I turn my head to track his movement as he stretches to reach for the beach bag. After some digging, he takes out the wet wipes I grabbed in case we needed them, my small bullet vibrator, and a bottle of lube. I'm guessing these are the real surprises.

"When did you put those in there?" I ask.

"Oh, these?" he asks cheekily, holding the vibrator and lube up like prizes.

"Yes, those."

"Snuck them in while you were in the bathroom."

Anticipation builds in my stomach as he puts them beside us then brings his hands to my hips again, this time to undo the string ties of my bottoms. When the bows easily come undone, he maneuvers us so that he can slip them off me. My body is now splayed open for him with my left knee bent, giving him more space to play between my legs.

"Such easy access you gave me," he purrs, throwing my bottoms to the side and running his palms over the curves and dimples of my ass. "And your cunt is already dripping for me, you dirty girl." He emphasizes his point by swiping a finger over the mess I've made on my thighs before wiping it on my ass.

"Elijah," I moan breathlessly, pressing my forehead into my arm. "You're teasing me."

He spanks my ass lightly then grips the bare cheeks. "Good."

I huff into the towel, frustrated.

He chuckles. "Just relax, Alex. I'm going to make you feel good."

I want to tell him that he's already made me feel good then order him to get on with sticking his cock in me because I'm desperate for him, but I don't. And I'll admit, I'm curious about what he's planning. I hear the wet wipes opening, and I turn my head again to watch Elijah clean his hands and cock of sunscreen residue then do the same between the crease of my ass. I shiver at the cold wipe, my pussy getting wetter. Then he picks up the vibrator and cleans it off for good measure before turning it on.

He notices me watching him and holds up the buzzing bullet. "If anything gets to be too much or you want me to stop, tell me, understand?"

I nod my agreement. "What are you going to do?"

He moves so he's no longer on top of me but kneeling next to me. "Get on your forearms with your ass up," he commands.

More curious now, I do what he says. A warm breeze meets my wet pussy, making me press back in hopes that he'll touch me if I reach him. Instead, he puts the tip of the vibrator at the top of my ass then runs it down the seam until goosebumps break out over my skin.

"I'm going to get you ready to take my cock in your ass, Alex."

I let out a desperate sound at the dominance in his tone as he separates my cheeks with his hands and spits on the tight ring of muscles.

"Elijah!"

He presses his thumb against my hole like he did in the shower then replaces it with the tip of the vibrator.

"Oh god," I cry into the towel. My muscles push back against the intrusion and onslaught of sensations.

"Relax into the feeling," he says, running his free hand down the length of my back. "And remember to breathe."

"Okay," I whimper as he pushes the toy further in, dropping some lubricant alongside his spit to make it more slippery. "Oh, fuck," I cry as the wider part of the toy slips in. When I try to push it out, Elijah stops the forward movement and instead spins it around.

"You look so sexy like this, Alex, letting me use your body however I want." When I take a breath, he pushes it further in and ups the vibrations to the highest setting.

I groan as I absorb the feeling into my body. Elijah's hand is still stroking my ass and back, talking me through it.

"How does it feel?"

I let out a low hum. "It's different."

"Good or bad different?"

"Good. Or at least I think so."

He moves the toy in and out again, twisting it in a circle so that it feels like he's stretching me. It burns a little, but it doesn't feel bad. I kind of like it.

"Let me know if you need me to stop," he says, but I know I won't need to.

Once he has another verbal yes from me, Elijah continues playing. He teases me, using more pressure to stretch me wider, then he pushes the toy back in, messing with the vibration settings. He continues to do this for I-don't-know-how-long, but with the gentle sound of the lake lapping at the shore and the birds chirping, I'm lulled into an almost meditative state.

My eyes close, and I breathe into the new feelings then start to imagine what it's going to feel like to take his cock there instead of the toy. I'll feel every ridge and vein of his length as I come around him, squeezing him.

I let out a low moan as Elijah palms my ass cheek, spreading me for him as he still plays. When I get to the point I'm relaxed and ready for him to get to the next part, the even more fun part, he drags a finger through my arousal, teasing the entrance to my vagina as he keeps moving the toy.

"Alex," he says, low and raspy as he fingers me. "Do you think this beautiful ass of yours can hold the toy in?"

I lick my lips, wondering why he wants me to keep it inside me. "I don't know."

"Will you try for me?"

I want to say I'd do anything for him, but instead, I nod and exhale a quiet *"Yes."*

"Good girl," he praises. "I'm going to let go now." When he does, I tighten my muscles, holding it. He molds both his palms to the globes of my ass then bites down on one of the cheeks like it's an apple.

"Elijah," I cry, my thighs starting to shake.

"Spread your knees wider for me, Alex. I want to see your pretty pink cunt dripping for me while you hold the vibrator in your ass."

With another needy sound, I slowly and carefully, while still gripping the vibrator as tight as I can, widen my knees, the sand pushing to the side under the towel. Elijah leaves his position as soon as I'm settled, but before I can ask him what he's doing, he gets under my legs so his face is directly beneath my pussy. Then he's pulling me down on top of him.

CHAPTER FOURTEEN

Elijah

I'M DROWNING IN ALEX'S perfect pussy, and I've never been happier. She moans wildly above me, her thighs shaking as I eat what's mine. Humming in satisfaction, I lap at her labia, her tangy arousal coating my tongue and lips like nectar.

Initially, I hadn't planned to eat her out quite yet, especially on the fucking sand. But when I saw her splayed open and ready for me, being the obedient and dirty girl that she is, I couldn't help myself.

The hands I have wrapped around her thighs pull the full weight of her down on my face, and I hold her there. I can hear her protests, but I'll have none of it. My lips wrap around her clit, and I suck hard.

"Elijah! Oh my god, oh my god," she chants as I devour her like she's my last meal. Something wet drops against my stomach, and I know she's released the vibrator, but I don't give a shit. I smack her ass playfully and pull away long enough to give her another command.

"Ride my face. I want you to soak me."

"Elijah, I don't—"

"You can do it, Alex." I swat her ass again. "Fuck my face." I pull her back down, feeling ravenous and almost out of control. I feel as if her taste on my tongue and the softness of her skin around me has lit a fuse in me, one that will cause me to explode if she doesn't give me what I need. What I crave.

With another suck to her clit, she starts to move, her pussy working over my mouth as I rain a few more light smacks on the globes of her ass. She cries out in pleasure, so I do it again, lapping at her folds now with the goal of licking her dry.

"Yes, Elijah, yes! Just like that, baby. I'm so close."

I wrap my lips back around her sensitive bud then flick my tongue in small motions, sliding one of my hands on her backside until I feel the slippery ring of muscle that I plan to fuck. She makes a low keening noise as I press a finger inside while keeping pressure on her clit.

"I'm coming! Oh my god." A hoarse cry leaves her as she continues to ride my face, her hips undulating in a choppy motion as she orgasms. I hold her steady as her arousal floods onto my lips and soaks my beard. *Fuck*. I think this is one of the best moments of my life, and I know I'm going to want to do this again before our weekend is up.

I lick and suck Alex through her release, my finger remaining planted inside her back entrance. My cock throbs, and my skin itches in anticipation of being inside her, watching my cum drip from her after I unload myself into her tight hole. God, my thoughts have turned incredibly filthy. "Mr. Serious" is no longer anywhere in my body.

When Alex is done shaking, I push up on her hips and remove myself from underneath her. Her head is resting on her forearms, chest pressed into the towel, her skimpy bikini top askew from her movements with her ass still in the air. I don't bother to wipe my mouth as I remove my trunks from my body, my erection bobbing free.

"Are you okay?" I check in with her, palming her ass and running my hands across her low back.

She exhales a chuckle that makes me think she's flying higher than a kite. "I think I'm in orgasm heaven."

My ego expands as I take my cock in my hand, pumping it a few times before placing it at the entrance to her cunt, gathering her wetness so I can use it as a natural lubricant. She moans when she feels my thick head dip inside her, but I don't let her savor it. I'm not fucking her there right now, even though it's tempting.

I reach to the side and grab the lube, squirting some on her tight rosebud that pulses lightly in anticipation. I could probably enter her with her arousal alone, but I don't want to make her first time uncomfortable. With one hand still jacking my cock, I use my other hand to dip the lube inside, feeling her muscles contract around my finger. When she moans and pushes back, I add another finger and then another.

"Remember to breathe, Alex." When she takes an inhale, I continue to stretch her, spending another minute making sure she'll be okay to take my girth. When I'm satisfied that she can, I pull back, replacing my fingers with the aching head of my cock.

"Are you ready?" I keep my tone low and soothing, though inside I feel as if I'm ready to snap. She looks over her shoulder at me, her lower lip trapped between her teeth as she nods.

"Fuck my ass, Elijah."

Her dirty, sex-laden permission is all I need to push inside her tight hole. Her back dips and arches as I move in an inch, watching her body accept my cock.

"Fuck." She moans into the towel, her thighs still quivering.

I feed another inch in, then another, and another. "That's it, dirty girl," I croon. "Exhale for me." When she does, I sink in more, the slippery heat of her constricting me.

"So big," she keens. "So full."

I rub my hand down her back, moving my hips as I curse at the feeling of her, at how well she's taking me. "Yes, Alex. Jesus, you're so hot like this. Your body was made for me."

At my words, she pushes her ass back, my cock sinking all the way in. We both shout together when I bottom out, my balls slapping against her sex. With my hands on her hips, I pause for a moment, letting her adjust. I squeeze and soothe her plush skin as I wait for her breathing to even out.

"Elijah," she murmurs, tone laced with need.

"Are you ready for me to fuck this sweet ass of yours, my dirty girl?"

"Yes. Please, yes. I need it, baby."

My cock twitches inside her, and I let my carnal need to pump her full of me take over. I pull back, watching my messy cock slide in and out.

Alex exhales a low sound of pleasure, and I pull almost all the way out before slamming back in. "*Ohhh!*" she cries.

I do it again, lifting her hips up so I can go deeper, my balls slapping against her at just the right angle so that she wails loudly, telling me to give her more. I plunge in and out as her cries become almost a musical soundtrack, one I'd love to play on repeat for the rest of my life.

"Elijah," she murmurs, her voice cracking as if she's teetering on the brink of orgasm again.

My grip on her hips is almost bruising now as I pull back and thrust all the way in again. Her body moves from the force of it. A shiver works up my spine, and my brow pinches, my release coming fast and quick.

I piston my hips and tug her back again, then I smack her ass, loving the way her freckled skin moves and turns shades of red and pink.

"I'm going to come," I grunt, my movements turning shallower.

"Yes, baby, I want to feel you," Alex begs.

"I'm going to show you who you belong to, Alex. I'm going to come in your tight ass till my seed is dripping out of you. And you're going to take it like a good wife should."

A shocked gasp leaves her mouth, but then she chants out several yeses as I lean my body forward. I slide my hand around her hips to find her clit. When I connect with the sensitive bud, she screams out, and I continue to fuck her deep, the muscles of my ass flexing.

"I'm coming, Elijah. Fuck, I'm coming again," she moans.

My eyes close as the myriad of sensations take over. My hand on her clit, her heated skin against mine, the particles of sand on our bodies, and my cock deep in her ass, the muscles contracting as I fuck her.

With a final strum of my fingers on her clit and a thrust of my hips, my orgasm hits me at the same time Alex falls over the edge. My release paints her insides. I curse, feeling her pussy flutter through the barrier between us.

"Oh my god, baby. I can feel you coming inside me. I can feel you," she moans as I collapse forward, making sure not to hurt her as I continue to rut into her, fucking any cum that's slipped out back inside her.

"Take it, Alex. Take all of me," I say against her ear. Her body shudders as my release pumps into her, taking everything I give.

It seems like our orgasms go on forever, but when my body finally stops shaking and my cock is spent, I kiss her shoulder and slowly back off her body. When I slip my softening length free, my cum spills out along with the lube I used.

"So pretty." I smack her ass lightly. "My dirty wife."

Alex releases a long and satisfied sigh, and my half-hard cock twitches, new images popping up behind my eyelids at doing the same to her pussy. At using her body and making it mine every single day for the rest of our lives.

For a second, I stun myself at the thought. Then I blink to remind myself this isn't real. That I have only one night and part of tomorrow with this woman.

With a final palm of her ass, I grab the wet wipes with unsteady hands and pull a few out. After I've cleaned the mess of us off my length, I go to wipe the remnants of my cum from her, but Alex stops me by turning and lying flat on her back.

"Leave it," she says, a slow smile on her face. "I want to feel you for as long as I can."

I grin lazily at how dirty this woman is, how perfect. I drop the wet wipes to the side before crawling up her body to give her a kiss. She opens to me without hesitation, and I slowly stroke her tongue, exploring every inch of her mouth. After a time, I pull away, flopping to the side, both of us spent and sated. I look up at the clouds in the sunny sky as she snuggles into me.

"Still hate the beach?" she asks, green eyes sparkling.

"Yes." I smirk. She smacks my chest, and I grab her hand, moving my thumb over some of the sand that's accumulated on her now sweaty skin. "Though I can't say I hate beach anal."

A laugh bursts from her lips, and then she tugs her hand from mine, sitting up. "Let's go swim. We can wash off all the sand"—she waggles her eyebrows—"and other things." She glances toward her ass suggestively.

"You're going to be the death of me."

With a soft giggle, she stands, tugging her already half-off bikini top from her breasts so she's fully nude and on display for me.

"Then it will be a good death." She winks before running toward the lake, laughter trailing behind her as she splashes into the clear blue waters. "Come in! I promise I'll protect you from lake sharks, dear husband!"

I roll my eyes, but I get up and follow her into the water anyway. Because I'm realizing there's nothing I could deny Alex Martin. Not even at the risk of chafing sand and lake sharks.

Chapter Fifteen

Alex

"Oh my god!" I moan.

Elijah chuckles, his thumb pressing into the arch of my foot. "Feel good?"

I flop my head back against the couch and moan again. "Feel good? You're a master foot massager."

He digs his thumb in again. "Maybe I should make a career change."

My eyes connect with his sparkling blue ones, and for a moment, I'm stunned at how different he looks in such a short amount of time. The man I met yesterday was stressed, tense, and looked older. Not in a harsh way, in the way most people look when they're tired and overworked.

But this man in front of me is the opposite. No longer is the pinch in his brow permanent. He's relaxed, and his shoulders are even less tense. He looks well-rested despite our lack of sleep since last night, though we did take a short nap wrapped up together once we got back from the beach. I fell asleep almost immediately when my head hit the pillow, his warm chest pressed against my back. It was...*wonderful*. A feeling I could get used to.

Elijah grins, pushing some of his silver hair off his forehead. It's usually styled, but since we weren't planning on leaving the house, he left it a little shaggy after our shower. It's sexy as hell, and I can't stop myself from staring at him. Especially now that his skin is sun-kissed and he looks so...happy.

"Do I have some of your delicious dinner on my face?" he asks after another beat of me staring, referring to the steaks I made us.

I shake my head, his smile and compliment causing my heart to race. "No. I was just thinking that you may not like the beach, but the beach sure likes you. You're glowing."

His lips purse. "I'm not going to turn into a California beach boy, if that's what you're suggesting."

"I would never suggest that of you, Mr. Serious."

He tickles my feet, and I squeal, trying to pull from his grasp. He laughs at my futile attempts and continues to tickle me until I can't take it anymore.

"Uncle!" I cry playfully, kicking at him.

He grabs my legs to stop my flailing but gives into my pleas.

"Spoilsport," he chuffs before motioning for me to tuck into his side instead. I glare at him playfully but give in easily to his request, wanting to be closer to him. I shift myself so I can move under his open arm and rest my head on his shoulder. When I'm settled, he kisses the crown of my head. The simple action melts my insides, and I let my mind imagine that this is real. That Elijah is really my husband and this is our house.

I stare blankly at the television screen in front of us. A romantic comedy we haven't been paying attention to is playing softly. On the screen, a man is proposing to a woman, confessing his love for her.

"Do you think you'll get married again?" I ask Elijah, not really thinking of the words that just came out of my mouth.

His hand stops moving on my arm, and I dare to look into his eyes. I find myself stupidly worried about what I'll see there. I shouldn't care either way—I know this is supposed to be a one-weekend thing. I was the one who suggested it. But I wonder what his answer will be.

"Well." He smiles softly. "I'm already married."

My stomach flips. He's been very committed to our role play. And while I've loved every second of it, I've come to realize we're playing a very dangerous game here, one I'm starting to question if I can come back from. Because I really, really like when he calls me his wife.

"Okay, hypothetically, then. If we'd never gotten married, would you get remarried?"

He lets out a small puff of air then stares deeply into my eyes. My heart stops beating as he squeezes my arm. "I'd like to think that I will. That my dream of starting a family isn't that far away from reality. But I'm getting older, and the older I get, the less I think it would be fair for a child to have a parent who isn't as spry as I would've been had I had them at a younger age."

My heart aches when I hear the pain in his words, so I lean up and kiss him gently on the mouth. I want to say it's a good thing he's with me, then. That I can give him the life he wants, that we both want. But I know that would be a lie.

"Tell me," he says when I pull back. "Why did you decide to be a teacher instead of working for your dad's company?"

I rest my head back against his shoulder, interlacing one of my hands with his. "Shouldn't you have asked me that before we got married?" I tease him this time.

He smirks. "Okay, fair. But no time like the present, Wife. Spill."

I chuckle, squeezing his hand. "I don't know if you know this, but Stephanie is my stepmom."

He nods. "I did know that."

"My mom, Grace, was a teacher when she met my dad. He likes to tell me that she loved teaching almost as much as she loved me. He told me how she couldn't wait to go back to work when she went into remission. But then, her breast cancer spread before she could."

"I'm so sorry, Alex. That's terrible."

I press my lips together. "I was so young when she died, I don't remember her much. I'm lucky, because Stephanie has been a wonderful mom to me. But when it came time to pick a career, I knew I wanted to follow in my mom's footsteps.

Like her, I love kids. I've always wanted a big family, and I like working in education. Shaping young minds and all that." I grin. "I've never really been into what Dad does, though I know a part of him wishes I did. And who knows? Maybe someday I'll change paths, but I'm happy teaching right now. Even if it's hard a lot of the time."

"I admire you," Elijah murmurs, kissing the crown of my head once more.

I look up at him, only seeing truth in his eyes. "You do?"

"You forged your own path, even though it would've been somewhat easier for you to work for Oliver. You had a built-in path, and you chose to take a new one. That takes a lot of guts, Alex. Ones I wish I had."

My gaze turns questioning. "What do you mean?"

A sad smile plays at his lips. "I've lived my life how my father wanted me to. He was very old school and strict. He instilled in me that I had to get good grades, go to college, get a degree, get a job that paid well, get married. But if I had done what I wanted to do, I think I would've chosen a different career path and not gotten married to the first woman he approved of."

I study him thoughtfully. "Would you be writing novels instead?"

"Maybe. Or at least doing something a bit more on the creative side. Like you, I take after my mother. She loved art, books, and watching classic films. I suppose that all rubbed off on me during my childhood. But my father hated it and always made sure I was on the path he wanted instead."

I frown. "Why is that?"

"As I mentioned, my father was an old-school man. He worked hard to make a good life for our family. He viewed a possible career in the arts as a weakness, something I should not even consider. He believed art was only worthwhile if it was an investment of some sort or a way to flex your wealth. It's why I enjoy paintings and architecture and another reason Oliver wanted me to come here for the weekend to stay in this house."

He smiles softly at that.

"Those art mediums became an easy way to enjoy that part of myself without having my father question it, though I've always written on the side, keeping my stories secret. Only my mother knew about them. And well, now you." He squeezes my hand. "That's why I'd love to publish a book someday, for her. And of course, for me. To say I finally did something I wanted to do."

My heart squeezes in my chest at everything he told me, attempting to process it all. The fact that it seems he's never done anything just for himself, that he told me about his writing. That he's telling me about his parents now and what seems to be all these secret parts of himself.

"Are your parents not with us anymore?" I ask quietly. I hold my hands steady in his as he grips them tighter.

"Yes. Both in the last five years."

"I'm so sorry."

He shakes his head. "Don't be. I wish they could have been around longer, but they lived good lives. And despite my father's shortcomings, he was a good man, even if he made me angry often. He did the best he could. Same with my mother."

I try desperately to keep the tears from my eyes and hold it together. But all I want to do is throw my arms around Elijah and hug him, to ease all the pain and loneliness I see hidden beneath his soft smile. But I manage to hold back. I stroke my thumb over the top of his hand instead.

"You know, I used to do more creative writing at Spark until I took the promotion Oliver offered me. I still do some but not a lot. I enjoyed it."

My eyes brighten at the change of tone in his voice while revealing that. "If I know my dad, I know that if you told him that, he'd work with you to create a role better suited for you—or at least adapt the one you have now. I may not have known he was talking about you when he talks about his friend "Astor," but I know he loves and admires you. He sent you to this house for a weekend to get some rest and relaxation and knew you would enjoy it because you like art and architecture. That shows me even more how much he cares for you. You should talk to him."

Elijah strokes the pads of his fingers up and down my arm, his eyes unfocused. "You're giving me a lot to think about this weekend, Alex."

"Is that a good or a bad thing?"

He turns his gaze back to me. "I think it's a good thing."

I snuggle into him and turn my attention back to the screen where the couple is now getting married. My imagination takes over as I picture what a wedding to Elijah would be like. When I planned to marry Sean, it was going to be a big affair in my mind, with hundreds of dad's friends and employees and of course, all of Sean's. It was going to be lavish and probably in a five-star hotel because that's what Sean liked.

I turn my attention to Elijah's bearded jawline, the light from the TV reflecting on his masculine features. If we were to get married in real life, I think it would be in a little chapel somewhere with old stained glass windows casting rainbows on my white dress and only our close friends and family. I'd say the beach, but something tells me he wouldn't like the sand between his toes. Maybe I could convert him.

That has me smiling.

Elijah feels my gaze on him and looks down into my eyes. "You're staring at me again."

"Just thinking."

"About what, my sweet wife?" He grins.

My mouth opens, ready to tell him that I'm thinking yet again of what it would be like if this was real. If we could both come home from work every night to each other. From our time together so far, I know I would cook him meals, then we would do the dishes together before we settled in for the night. He'd rub my feet since I stand all day while we debriefed our time apart before he'd take out the trash, then we'd brush our teeth together side-by-side.

Afterwards, I'd thank him for being such an amazing and attentive husband by letting him come inside me each night. I'd let him fill me with him until we had miniature versions of us running around the house.

But instead, I squeeze his hand and grin back at him. "How lucky I am to have met you."

His eyes soften, and he kisses my forehead. "I'm lucky to have met you, too, Alex."

I press a kiss to his T-shirt-clad chest then rest my head over his heart, trying to enjoy the present with him. And praying that, by some miracle, it doesn't have to end.

Chapter Sixteen

Elijah

"That's it, my dirty girl, come around my cock. Show me that you belong to me." Alex's nails score down my back, and I pump into her relentlessly, the mattress shifting back and forth from the power of my thrusts.

"You feel so good, Elijah!" she cries, clutching me to her. "Don't stop—please, don't stop."

I change my angle and thrust into her deeper, trying to memorize the way she feels, the way she smells of roses. The way her cries sound and how her lips move against mine as I kiss her. I nip at her lips and press my forearms into the mattress on either side of her head, seating myself as deep as I can inside her.

"Fuck, Alex. You feel good, too. I don't want to stop."

She throws her head back as I thrust against her G-spot. "Then don't stop!"

But I don't think she understands what I meant when I said it. The mid-afternoon sun is already getting lower in the sky, signaling it's past time for our departure, meaning this is our last time together. But I don't want it to be.

Alex's pussy squeezes around me, and my brain snaps me back to the moment, back to me being inside my beautiful "wife." I need to focus, to brand this moment into me so I never forget it. I slow down my thrusts, and she whines, her perfect green eyes opening in question.

God, she makes a beautiful picture, her freckled cheeks flushed, her ginger hair spread out and tangled from my hands gripping it tightly while I fucked her from behind before this.

"Why did you slow down?"

I grin at her need for me. Instead of answering, I kiss her nose then her cheeks, letting my tongue trace a cluster of freckles on her skin before sealing my mouth over hers. When I pull back from the kiss, I remove my cock before sheathing myself slowly back in. Each time I thrust, I change my pace. Fast, then slow, then slower and faster.

"Elijah," she purrs, her fingers gripping my waist as she tries to pull me in deeper.

"So impatient, so greedy," I tease, moving my hips in a slow circle.

In answer, she slides her hands lower to grip my ass. "I know this is our last time, Elijah," she says breathlessly, "but please, baby. I need you to fuck me hard. Make me feel you. Come so deep inside me you'll drip out of my pussy for days."

My cock pulses, and I stare deeply into her eyes. Her words may have said one thing, but I know what she meant. She wants to feel me for as long as possible so that after we're gone from here, from this place, she has a reminder of me.

I bring my lips down to hers, my tongue licking into her mouth as she removes her hands from my body. She slides her arms up the bed and gets me to take her hands in mine. My forearms are now pressing hers into the mattress with our hands linked.

Pulling back from the kiss, I rest my forehead against hers as our gazes lock. My thrusts get stronger, and the mattress shifts from the force of me. I don't know when the atmosphere changes, but as I look into her eyes, her short breaths puffing against my cheek, I know that I'm leaving here a changed man.

"Elijah," she says huskily as I hit her G-spot again and again. "I'm going to come."

"Then come, my dirty girl. Take what's yours."

She bites her lip and nods her head. A single thrust of my hips draws another release from her sensitive and overused body, one I've made sure to play with since the moment we woke up this morning.

"Elijah!" she cries, my name departing from her lips with devout reverence as she falls endlessly over the edge, her tight pussy pulsing around my cock so hard I have no choice but to follow her over.

I come, my body sagging against hers as I empty everything, every drop I have left, inside her. I paint and fill her body exactly how I know she loves. How I love...

Alex exhales a shaky laugh, her hand untangling from mine to brush back some of my hair before trailing a finger down my cheek. We stay connected like that for a time, my cock still inside her, our bodies pressed together as if we're both trying to lock this final time into our memories.

When a phone chimes in the background, it startles both of us. Alex sighs, tracing a finger over my lips. "Reality is calling," she says. But she makes no move to get up.

"What if we just stayed here?" I muse. "Do you think anyone would notice we're gone?"

Another chime of a phone, and she groans. "That's my mom's text tone. She probably wants to know if I'm on the road yet."

I drop my forehead to Alex's clavicle and leave an open-mouthed kiss on it before I finally roll off of her. She sighs, her eyes closing as she lays there, making a mess on the towel we laid down for that specific reason. Unable to help myself, I drop my hand between her legs, brushing the pads of my fingers over her sensitive clit until I reach her entrance. Alex lets out a small whimper, propping herself up so she can watch me push every drop of my cum back in.

"Elijah," she says quietly, her voice sad as our eyes meet. "What if we..." But she doesn't finish the sentence.

I drag my hand up her body and take hold of her hand. "We can't, Alex," I say, knowing what she was going to say. *What if we tried to make this work?*

She looks at my hand then into my eyes. My heart breaks at the turmoil I see there, as if, with those three words, I've crushed all her hope. But we can't be together. She knows that. No matter how much I'd love to go back to LA and make her mine, properly date her and show her off to anyone and everyone, to tell Oliver I don't give a fuck what he thinks and be with his daughter, I can't. My life is too wrapped up with the Martins between my job and being Oliver's friend.

Alex's phone chimes yet again, and she pulls her hand away from mine. The way she holds tension in her body for the first time since I've met her tells me our time here is done. With that simple statement, I've ended our weekend of make-believe.

"I'm going to shower," she says, using the towel to wipe between her legs before she stands. I sit on the mattress, unable to move, knowing that this is her way of saying I'm not allowed in the shower with her. That what we had is over now.

"Alex," I say, stopping her. "I wish things were different, that we had met under different circumstances."

Her eyes lift to mine, and she smiles sadly. "It's okay, Elijah. I knew what this was. You were clear with me from the beginning. I made you an offer, and I meant what I said. I'll get over it."

I swallow. *I'll get over it.* I don't know if she means her words, but they sting, nonetheless. I know I deserve them. Because Alex Martin is the kind of woman who deserves more than I can give her. She deserves a man who isn't a coward. A man who doesn't worry what his friends and coworkers would think. And she deserves better than a man who hasn't quite figured out what he wants at forty-five years old.

"I'm sorry, Alex," I say, but she waves me off, putting her shoulders back and erasing any visible sadness from her features.

"You have nothing to be sorry for." She takes a step forward and bends so she can lay a lingering kiss on my lips. "Thank you for an amazing weekend. I hope you find what you're looking for, Elijah."

My mind is screaming at me to say I already found it, to tell her I want this to be more than just a weekend of playing house, but the rational side of my brain won't let me.

"Alex," I say, trying to find more words to give her, but she silences me with another gentle kiss.

"I'll see you downstairs." Then she pulls away and walks into the bathroom, clicking the door shut behind her.

Chapter Seventeen

Alex

One Month Later

"Alex, honey, you look stunning," Mom says.

"Thanks." I smooth my hands down the sides of my shimmering black cocktail dress that hugs all my curves as we walk toward the doors of one of the fanciest hotels in downtown Los Angeles.

"I know you've been so busy with the start of the school year, but it means so much to your dad that you agreed to come to this event. We both know how much you hate them."

I force a smile to my lips as the sliding doors open and we walk into the brightly lit foyer. "You know I wouldn't miss tonight," I say truthfully.

While I hate going to my dad's work events and have managed to skip out on them for most of my adult life, I know this one means a lot to him. He's getting a prestigious award for being an innovator in the creative media space, one he worked hard to get.

"You know who else is going to be here?" Mom smiles.

My stomach drops as we get directed to the ballroom where the event is taking place. "Please don't tell me it's that stuck-up hotelier you asked me to give a second date to?"

She lets out a high-pitched laugh. "No, no. Though I still think you should give Brad a second chance."

I wrinkle my nose. Anyone named Brad only gets one chance in my book. "He was over thirty minutes late to our date last week and used a fork to pick chicken from between his teeth. Who does that?"

"Okay, fine. You're right. But I'm not talking about Brad."

"Please tell me it's not another man you're trying to set me up with?"

"I wish, but no. Elijah will be here—we should be sitting at a table with him."

My steps falter, and the hair rises on the back of my neck. "Oh, that's nice of him to come," I say, hoping my voice doesn't sound too squeaky.

"He insisted when your dad told him. I know you guys spent time together last month at the lake house. I can't believe your dad and I did that to you both. I'm still so embarrassed."

I take a shallow breath, trying not to flush. "It's fine. We made do."

She smiles at me, completely oblivious that when I say "made do" I mean we fucked all over her beloved lake house for an entire weekend. My thighs clench together at the memory.

"I'm sure he'll be happy to see you. Your dad said he's a completely different man since he came back. Says his spirit is lighter. He leaves work on time now and even asked if he could take on some more creative work, reshape his role a bit."

"Oh?" I ask curiously as we walk through the entrance to the ballroom. Voices and music drift around us as glassware clinks loud in my ears.

"Yes. Normally, your dad doesn't talk much about him, says their guy time is sacred or something, but he wants to offer Elijah the lake house more often. Says it's good for his business." She laughs.

My stomach turns as we walk further inside. I should be glad that Elijah is doing more of what he wanted. That he's happy. It seems he took my advice and spoke to my dad about his position at the company. But a selfish part of me was hoping he'd be miserable, missing me like I've missed him.

For the last month, I've tried anything and everything not to think about him, even going on that horrendous date with Brad. But I can't seem to shake him. Elijah's literally burned himself into my corneas. Into my skin. I swear, every man I see with gray hair is him. And when I close my eyes at night, I gaze into his sapphire-blue ones and feel his warm hands caressing my body.

I swallow the lump in my throat. "That's good. I think I'm going to stop at the bar before I sit. Do you want something?"

"Sure, honey. A white wine would be lovely. Your dad texted that he's backstage right now talking to the organizer but will be out in a minute."

"Sounds good."

Mom walks off, and I don't bother to see where she goes. I'm sure I'll be able to spot her and Elijah's silver hair from a mile away.

Thankfully, the bar line isn't long, and I'm quickly at the front of the line.

"I'll take the best red you have and a chardonnay," I tell the bartender with a smile. He's cute with short blond hair and dimples. He's probably around my age or a tiny bit younger.

He smiles at me, revealing a row of straight white teeth. "I'm afraid the best red I have is an overly warm blend."

I cringe. "Didn't spring for the good stuff, huh?"

"Not with wine, at least. But I can offer you some nice vodka, or I hear the champagne isn't too bad."

I debate taking a shot but then decide against it. My stomach is already nervous because I know Elijah will be here. I don't want to make it worse or get drunk and accidentally let my dad know I slept with his best friend.

My body grows hot. "I'll suffer with the overly warm blend."

"I respect that choice," the bartender says. He pulls out two glasses and pours the cold chardonnay first before doing mine.

"You come to these things often?" he asks, his eyes moving up and down my body as he slides the wine glasses forward.

"No, not really. Do I look like I do?" I ask, attempting to keep my voice level so he doesn't think I'm flirting with him.

"You fit in." He looks down my dress again, lingering longer than I'd like when he reaches my cleavage. "Though it seems like you don't want to be here."

I pull open my clutch and grab a tip for him, feeling slightly uncomfortable now. "Thanks for letting me know. I'll have to work on my poker face."

As I put the tip down on the bar and reach for my drinks, his hand shoots out and rests on top of mine. "My break is in fifteen minutes if you want to talk more."

My eyes narrow at the audacity of this man. But before I can say anything, a warm, steady hand is on my back and the tickle of a beard is in my ear.

"Please remove your hand from my wife," a familiar baritone voice warns.

The bartender's touch disappears as the hair on my arms stands on end. I don't have to turn my head to know who has come to my rescue, who would dare to call me his wife.

"I'm sorry, sir. I didn't see a ring," he says, holding up his hands.

"Ring or not, your behavior is uncalled for."

The heat in my body rises from embarrassment and arousal. I shouldn't be aroused, but I can't help it. Elijah is here. He's touching me. He called me his wife. I indulge in the comfort of his masculine body for a moment, enjoying the familiarity and safety I feel in his arms. The pressure of his hand on my back deepens, and my heart beats faster in my chest.

"Ladies and gentlemen, please grab a drink and take a seat. We'll start the ceremony in about fifteen minutes," the emcee's voice says over the loudspeaker.

I stiffen, and I blink, remembering where we are. We're in public. My parents are here. People, including my mom and dad, could be watching. I put space between me and Elijah and grab the drinks off the bar top.

"I'm sorry," the bartender says. "I really thought—"

"It's fine," I cut him off, needing to get out of this situation. I bump Elijah with my shoulder. "Come on. Let's go to our table."

My voice snaps Elijah out of his stare down with the bartender. He looks at me, his azure gaze drinking me in as if he fully noticed that I was standing there, that I'm real.

"Let me take those," he says, reaching for the drinks.

"I've got them." I smile, my cheeks tense.

At my refusal to let him help me, his jaw clenches. Anger rises in my belly, flushing my chest and my cheeks. His eyes watch it happen, and I see him lick his lips. Elijah reaches out and touches my arm, and I swear my entire body lights on fire.

"Alex," he whispers.

I shake my head, unwilling to trust my voice. I'm at war in my mind right now. One part of me wants to take him into a dark corner and mold my body against his, to kiss the lips I've missed so much the last month. But then another part of me wants to yell at him for being a Neanderthal, for staking his claim on me in public when he's made it clear what our weekend was: just one weekend. Which I couldn't and wouldn't fault him for. But then he goes and calls me his wife the first time he sees me?!

"We should get to the table," I snap, walking briskly away from him.

Trying to ignore Elijah's presence at my back, I walk through the crowd, eventually spotting my mom's blonde head and my dad's gray hair. I'd recognize him anywhere because he's got a small bald spot at the top that Mom's been trying to get him to "take care of," aka get hair plugs or a toupee. But Dad will hear nothing of it. He says aging is cool and hip now. I don't know if that's true, but that's Oliver Martin for you. He walks to the beat of his own drum.

"Alex," Elijah says as we get closer to the table, but I don't turn to look at him. "We should talk."

I shake my head. "Not here."

He sighs, but I don't know what he expects. He wanted to keep our relationship a weekend thing, and I respected that. I also don't want to ruin my dad's night. Because finding out his best friend and I fucked at his lake house isn't exactly something a person reveals at an awards function. Or ever.

Mom's head turns as I approach. "There you are!"

At her proclamation, Dad's head turns, too. "Look who it is! We were wondering if you got lost."

I force a smile for my parents while I hand Mom the now sweating glass of chardonnay. "Sorry, I picked up a stray at the bar," I say.

They both notice Elijah at the same time, and their grins broaden. "Well, well. You clean up nice, you son of a gun," Dad says, standing to greet Elijah with a handshake and a man hug.

"You don't look too bad yourself, Martin." Elijah pats his back. While he looks normal and happy, I can see his pinched brow from here, showing me his signs of distress. I want to walk over and smooth it away; instead, I grip my wine glass as Dad steps away from Elijah to hug me.

"You look beautiful, honey," he says, giving me a kiss on the cheek. "Thank you for coming."

"I wouldn't miss it."

After Mom hugs Elijah, we all sit. Thankfully, it's a round table, and Elijah is sitting next to my dad while I'm on the other side next to my mom. There are three empty chairs between us. At first, I thought it was a good thing we weren't next to each other, but now he's in my direct line of sight to the stage, so I have no choice but to stare at him.

Dad's right—he does look nice. Who am I kidding? He looks more than nice. His silver hair and salt-and-pepper beard are styled perfectly, and the black fitted suit he's wearing looks as if it was tailored for his body. The masculine and lean body I've imagined lying on top of mine every night. The body I've craved to hold me.

I cross my legs under the table and take a sip of my wine, hoping a little alcohol will soothe my nerves. I cringe at the flavor—the bartender was right. It's too warm. It's also just not good.

"Not to your liking?" Elijah's question reaches my ears.

I flush at his words, my eyes darting to my parents. They don't think anything funny of the comment, and why would they? To them, it seems like he's simply making conversation. But all I'm thinking of is my dinners with Elijah. Of our time in the hot tub when I had the taste of merlot and his cum on my tongue. And by the secret smile tugging at the corner of his lips, he's thinking of it, too.

"It's fine," I say, taking another sip, though I can't hide my grimace.

Dad chuckles. "You have a delicate palette, Alex. Elijah, you should see my girl at the vineyards in Napa. She gives every sommelier a run for their money."

I flush. "I'm not that good, Dad."

"I beg to differ. You're remarkable," Elijah says almost too quickly, making my parents blink at him in confusion.

My now fully red cheeks combined with my wide-eyed stare has him recognize his error. He takes a sip of the water in front of him before he says, "Alex was kind enough to teach me about wines when we were at the lake house."

"Oh, yes." Dad smiles, his shoulders relaxing. "I keep forgetting about that accident."

"I swear Oliver and I talk to each other," Mom says to Elijah. "I'm the one who keeps track of who is staying when, and I thought it would be free for Alex to take."

"It's okay, Stephanie," Elijah says. "It was nice to have company."

"You never did say what you did that weekend," Dad says, taking a sip of what looks like whiskey while bouncing his gaze between Elijah and me.

I didn't say because I knew I could never keep a straight face. My gut wrenches, and I wish more than anything I wouldn't have come tonight. Had I known Elijah would be here, I would have faked sick or something to avoid this exact moment.

"I told you about it, Oliver. We mostly spent time separately except for meals when Alex offered to cook."

I close my eyes for a brief moment, thinking of our meals together that weekend, how we fell so easily into a routine with each other. I haven't cooked much since then, not only because I've been short on time with work but because it reminds me too much of him.

"Right, right," Dad says. "I remember you saying that now." But by the way he continues to look between me and Elijah, I feel like he knows something. Which would be impossible. It's not like he had cameras inside the house. Do I have "I fucked your best friend and VP" stamped across my forehead?

Just as it seems like Elijah is about to say something, Mom interrupts. "Oh look, Alex. Brad is here."

Goosebumps break out over my arms—not from the mention of Brad alone, but from Elijah's intense stare. Thankfully, Dad's eyes are following Mom's, and they are ignoring us. I swallow, diverting my focus away from a steely Elijah.

"You should go say hi to him," my mom says, and I purse my lips.

Dad chuckles when he sees my sour face. "Stephanie, darling, stop trying to set her up with Brad. You know how poorly that date went. Plus, I don't like him, either."

Mom whacks his shoulder. "You don't like anyone for Alex."

Dad takes another sip of his drink, his eyes smiling at me. "That's because nobody is good enough for my little girl." When he puts his drink down, he turns his attention to Elijah, who is now looking quite pale. "When you have kids, Astor, you'll get what I'm saying. You'll want to murder anyone who even looks at your child wrong."

Elijah swallows, his Adam's apple bobbing on his cleanly shaven throat. Thankfully, the awkward moment is broken by the lights dimming and the emcee's voice over the loudspeaker welcoming everyone to the awards. Dad's focus goes to the stage, and he says something to Elijah that I can't hear.

I pick up my wine glass and pray his award is early on so I can fake a stomachache and leave before they serve the food. While the man onstage talks about innovation and the hard work it takes to be an entrepreneur, I can't help but watch Elijah's side profile. He's paying attention to the awards, but I can see his jaw clenched and brow pinched from here. He's most likely remembering what my mom said about my dad not liking anyone for me. He's probably convincing himself that he was right for keeping what we had to one weekend.

As I reach for my water, Stephanie leans over and whispers in my ear.

"Honey, did something happen between you and Elijah?"

My mouth turns to sandpaper. "What?" I say, attempting to keep my voice level and very quiet. "Why would you ask that?"

"Call it a mother's intuition."

I give her the *Are you joking?* look, and she sighs, saying even quieter now, "And you keep giving each other funny looks."

Busted. God, I'm bad at this. I want to lie to Mom, but I know that if I do, she'll see right through it. I've never been that great of a liar.

"We can't talk about this here," I say as Dad looks over at us.

"Everything okay?" he wonders quietly.

"Yes, dear." Mom smiles at him. "Just gossiping."

He grins and turns back to the awards. I dare a glance at Elijah, who's looking at me again, but then he quickly turns away. Crap, this is bad. As I'm about to excuse myself to the restroom so I can breathe, Dad says, "This is me."

Thankful for the distraction, I try to give my full concentration to the announcer and another woman who came up onstage to talk about my dad's achievements. Eventually, they call him up to the stage, and he stands, kissing Mom on the head and beaming at us before he walks off to collect his award.

With my dad no longer at the table, I fail in my attempt to keep my focus from Elijah and shift my eyes back to him. As if he can sense it, he turns his head, and we stare at each other. I try to convey to him that I think Stephanie knows, but his blue eyes remain steady. God, I wish I could speak mind to mind with him, to tell him I think our secret isn't so secret anymore. And if it is, it won't be for long.

Mom clears her throat loud enough that Elijah and I both break our connection and look to her. "When Oliver gets back, go to the bathroom, Alex. And you"—she commands Elijah—"go get a drink. Then you both can talk." She scans the room and motions with her head to a side door. "Go all the way down the hall and to the left; there's a veranda outside. He won't find you there."

Elijah's mouth drops open like a fish out of water. I shrug at him because what else can I do? He's probably thinking I told her, but I haven't said a word. Apparently, we really suck at pretending everything was just a normal weekend at the lake house.

Mom smiles softly at me. A smile that says whatever is going on is okay. I should've known that she wouldn't care if Elijah and I spent more than platonic time together. She's always been supportive of me, no matter what I've chosen to do—or *who* I've chosen to do. She even supported me in my relationship with Sean, though I knew she didn't like him, either.

I gulp down the rest of my disgusting wine and force my attention back to the stage. Dad is happy as he holds his award and launches into his speech, talking about the work he loves to do and why he does it. I love seeing him like this. My stomach twists, bile rising in my throat, and I start to think that maybe Elijah was right after all; we can't tell my dad. But now that Mom sort of knows, he has to find out eventually, right? I doubt she would be able to keep that secret—at least not for long.

I observe Elijah. He's worried and confused, and I don't blame him. I am, too. When the clapping starts, I take a deep breath and spot my dad as he comes back to the table. Mom is the first to hug him, then I get up and do the same. Elijah claps him on the back as he sits down and sets the fancy glass award on the table.

"Beautiful speech, Oliver," Mom says, leaning over to kiss him on the cheek. "I'm so proud of you."

"Thank you." Dad smiles, picking up the award. "I can use this as a fancy door stop."

I roll my eyes, and Elijah chuckles. With a sip of my water, I decide it's now or never. Part of me wants to run away from this, but with Stephanie peering at me and Elijah fidgeting as if he might crawl out of his skin, I know I need to face the proverbial music.

"Please excuse me; I'm going to use the restroom," I say, standing. I give Dad a small smile, and he mirrors it while Stephanie tries to reassure me with a gentle look. My gaze skips over Elijah, not wanting to draw any attention to us.

I brush my hands down my black dress as I weave my way through the tables and people until I'm outside the ballroom. I turn right and go down the hallway, taking the directions Mom gave me until I meet the doors of the veranda. They automatically slide open, and I'm greeted by the cool night air.

Turning to the left, I walk down the long porch until I'm the furthest I can possibly be from the doors. Once I'm satisfied with the distance, I lean against the white railing and take a deep breath.

Then I wait for Elijah.

CHAPTER EIGHTEEN

Elijah

MY BREATH LEAVES MY body as I spot Alex at the end of the veranda. She's leaning on the white railing, her ginger hair spilling over her shoulders in perfectly styled waves.

I don't move for a minute, letting my gaze linger while I take in her beauty. I absorb the image of her, drinking in the fact that she's real. She's here. And she's not a figment of my dreams anymore.

God, I've missed her. I've missed everything about her—her smile, her laugh, her voice, her teasing jokes and dirty mouth—I've missed it all. She's all that I've been able to think about. And the minute I saw her at the bar, I couldn't stop myself from walking over to her. She was a flame, and I was a moth. I'm helpless when she's around.

Sensing me staring, her head turns, and our eyes connect. That invisible string between us tugs, and I stick my hands in the pockets of my slacks as I walk to her. I'm glad nobody's out here but us so I can speak with her freely.

When I reach her, she turns so we're facing each other, her back pressed against the railing now. Her face is neutral, but I can see the stress in her body. I hate that I'm the one who's caused it.

"Hello, Alex," I say after a moment.

"Hi," she says back, her green eyes staring up at me through thick painted lashes.

"You look stunning." My gaze drags over her voluptuous form encased in a very tight and very short black cocktail dress.

She tucks some of her hair behind her ear. "Thank you. You look nice, too."

A smile tugs at my lips as silence envelops us. I think we're both unsure of how to start.

Eventually, Alex lets out a small sigh. "I didn't tell my mom anything, if that's what you're thinking."

"I'm not thinking that," I assure her.

"Well, she said we were looking at each other funny. And you didn't help matters with that wine comment. I think my dad got suspicious, too, if you didn't notice. But Elijah, I don't know what we're supposed to do now. My mom obviously knows something happened between us. I could ask her not to say anything, but I don't feel comfortable doing that. And what were you thinking telling that bartender I'm your wife? Anyone could have heard you!"

Alex's words spill out of her so fast I hardly have time to take them all in. When my brain catches up, I grasp her biceps and get her to look at me.

"Take a breath, Alex. Everything is going to be okay."

She scoffs and narrows her eyes at me. "What are you talking about? My dad is going to find out something happened between us, the very thing we wanted to avoid! Especially you."

"You're right. It was."

"You should've thought about that before you called me your wife in public and kept staring at me like you could see me without my clothes on!"

I can't help but smirk at her outburst. But then, her head cocks to the side as she registers my previous words.

"Wait, it *was*?" she asks. "What do you mean 'it was'?"

"When I heard you were going to be here tonight, I asked Oliver if I could still get a ticket. He thought it was to support him, which it was. I did and do always want to support him. But I wanted to see you."

"Um, what?" she asks, blinking up at me.

I release her arms and take a step forward, testing the boundaries between us. When she doesn't try to get away, I place my hands on the railing on either side of her, caging her in so our bodies meld together. A gentle gasp leaves her mouth, and I instantly feel as if my body has found its home again.

I inhale her rose scent and smile, our faces only inches apart. "Ever since we left the lake house, I can't stop thinking about you. I was an idiot to leave you that way. I was so caught up in what us being together would mean for my relationship with Oliver and my work that I didn't think of your feelings. Or my feelings, for that matter. I love Oliver like a brother, but I can't deny that what we have, Alex—it's special. It's not something I ever should've walked away from. It's been eating me up inside."

Her chest rises and falls in choppy movements. That red flush I love so much blooms up from the neckline of her dress and over her freckled chest.

"But Stephanie said you were doing well, that you took on more creative projects at work. That Dad thinks you should go to the lake house more often because of how different you were when you came back."

I stroke my knuckle down the side of her face. "You inspired me to start living my life the way I want, Alex. But it's not complete without you."

"Then why haven't you called or tried to contact me?"

"Because I'm a coward. And if I'm being honest, I thought you wouldn't want me after how we left things. But then Oliver brought you up, and I knew this was my chance to see you again. To talk with you, if you'd let me."

She swallows, her features tense. "And now, after calling me your wife and a few longing glances, you think I *do* want you?"

My heart thuds in my chest, and I drop my hand from her face. She's right. Just because I finally grew a pair doesn't entitle me to her. I was a fool to think that she'd simply walk back into my arms again after I explained myself. Maybe after we left, she realized the weekend was just a fun break from reality like we had originally planned it to be.

"Alex," I murmur. "I'm sorry for hurting you. And if you want me to walk away from this, I will. But I need you to know that if you still want to try to make this work, I'll walk in and tell Oliver right now that I'm in love with you."

Her green eyes go impossibly wide, and her mouth parts at my declaration. But I'm telling the truth. I know now that I loved her the first time I saw her. The last month away has only solidified my feelings. That time showed me that I wasn't just searching for what life had to offer me. I was searching for Alex.

"You love me?" she asks, her eyes glassy.

I dare to cup her cheek, my body relaxing when she leans into my touch. "I don't care if it sounds crazy, but I love you, Alex Martin. And I don't give a fuck if people don't like it."

"But your job?"

"I can always get a new job, Alex."

"And my dad?"

I step closer to her so our bodies are once again melded together. Then I speak very clearly to be certain she understands me. "If your dad loves either of us, he'll understand."

"And if he doesn't understand?"

"Then I'll leave it up to you to decide what you want to do. But either way, I'm in this with you, Alex, if you'll have me. I'll only walk away if you tell me to."

A tear drops down her cheek, and I catch it with my thumb.

"You'd really give up all that for me?" she asks after a moment, her voice watery.

I put my other hand on her cheek and rest our foreheads together. "I'd do anything for you, Alex."

"Then kiss me," she breathes out. "Show me how much you love me."

My heart hammers in my ears as I slide my fingers into her hair and grip the back of her head. I bring our lips together, sealing my mouth over hers, capturing the small moan that leaves her.

When Alex runs her tongue along the seam of my lips and dives into my mouth, something unlocks inside of us, and we become unleashed.

A month of being apart spills out of us, and I press her back into the railing, her breasts compressing against my chest as her hands find my waist, pulling me into her. Our tongues tangle, and the taste of her mixed with the notes of wine she drank overtakes my senses. I become drunk on her, the way she feels against me, the rose smell of her perfume, the softness of her skin. I don't know how I lasted a month away from her, but I never want to be without her again.

Alex's hands grip my ass, and she grinds into me. "Elijah," she exhales as she breaks our kiss. "Tell me you love me again."

I suck on the pulse point of her neck then kiss back up her throat. "I love you, Alex. I love you, I love you, I love you."

She groans a noise that goes straight to my cock, and then she's crushing her lips over mine, taking control of the kiss. She runs her hands up my back, pulling me closer as we grind against each other and make out like teenagers.

"I missed you, Mr. Serious," she says as we pull away for air. Her hand slips under the lapel of my suit coat, and then she's playing with the top of my leather belt.

"I missed you, too, dirty girl."

She grins wickedly at me, her fingers teasing my lower stomach through my shirt. I look around to see if anyone's here, but we're still alone.

Alex nips at my neck, and then I take her lips again. My hand runs down the plush curve of her waist, and when I meet the skin of her thigh, she whimpers into my mouth. She opens to me, and I consume her, her hand slipping under my belt buckle and our bodies moving against each other.

"I need you, Elijah," she pleads between kisses.

I move my hand to her neck and press my thumb into the column of her throat. "You have me."

She shakes her head. "No, I—"

"Elijah!" a booming voice yells.

Alex and I naturally jump apart from the scare, but I quickly recover and grab her hand. I turn my body to face who I already know is moving toward us.

"Let me handle him, okay?" Alex asks. We're both watching Oliver, who is angrily stalking toward us with a sympathetic-looking Stephanie trailing behind him.

I squeeze Alex's hand. "We'll handle him together."

She gives me a weak smile, looking thoroughly kissed and pink-cheeked. I'm fairly certain I'm wearing some of the pink lipstick that's missing from her lips, which will not help us in the slightest. But I can't find it within myself to care. I need my friend to understand that I love Alex. That he's going to have to get used to it.

"Get your hands off my daughter, Astor!" Oliver yells as he meets us.

"Oliver—" I start to say, but Alex steps in front of me and holds a calming hand up to him.

"Stop it, Daddy." He blinks at her as if her calling him "Daddy" instead of "Dad" has snapped him out of his rage. "Take a breath, and let's speak like adults," she warns evenly.

Pride swells in my chest, and I grip Alex's hand tighter. Oliver glances down at it then looks back up at us, his brow furrowed.

"Tell me what's going on, Elijah. Tell me why you're attacking my daughter!"

"Oliver!" Stephanie chides him. "Be reasonable."

"I am being reasonable! I'm the only sane person here right now!"

"Dad," Alex tries again. "Elijah wasn't attacking me. We're together."

Both Stephanie's and Oliver's mouths drop open a bit. But Stephanie seems more pleased than anything else, which surprises me. It's nice to know she'll be on our side in this.

"Together?! Have you lost your minds?" Oliver shouts.

Alex moves into my side, and I release her hand so I can wrap my arm around her shoulders. Then she speaks, her voice calm and sure. "I'm perfectly sane, unless being in love counts as insanity."

Stephanie sucks in a breath, and I think my best friend's head is about to pop off. But my heart is beating so loudly in my ears that I can't focus on his anger, because Alex said she's in love with me. Alex Martin is in love with me.

"In *love*?! Are you trying to kill me? Because I'm going to have a heart attack right now, Alex."

"Oliver, don't joke like that," Stephanie chides.

"I'm in love with Elijah, Dad. And you're not going to have a heart attack. Like I said, you're going to take a breath, and we're going to talk about this."

Oliver's fists clench at his sides. His green eyes are looking from Alex to me then to Stephanie then back to Alex again.

"Help me understand. I—" He pauses, his eyes connecting with mine once more. "You're my friend, Elijah. How could you?"

"I'm still your friend, Oliver. And we didn't do this to hurt you."

"No. A friend wouldn't do something like this," he says, his tone serious.

"Oliver, I—"

"How did this even happen?" He cuts me off, his cheek reddening.

"It happened at the lake house last month," Alex replies.

Oliver's lips press together, and he glares at me. "When Alex texted Stephanie of our mistake, I thought I could trust you to stay there and be a gentleman. Instead, you—you—" He huffs. "I trusted you with my daughter, Elijah."

"And you can still trust me with her. We did nothing wrong. We're consenting adults."

"You're fifteen years older than her!"

"Dad," Alex says, "I know this is hard for you to accept. You shouldn't have found out like this. But it's..." Alex looks up at me. "It's complicated."

"Have you been seeing each other behind my back this entire month?" Oliver asks after a moment. His tone is more level now but still filled with a disappointment that sours my stomach.

"No. Like I said, it's complicated. But you can trust Elijah, Dad. He's done nothing wrong. If anything, he's the one who was afraid of being with me because of your relationship. We both tried to stop something like this from happening, but..." Alex gazes at me again, her eyes warm and hopeful.

"But I was wrong to do that," I say firmly, pulling Alex into my side, trying to convey to her how much I need her, how sorry I am that this is happening this way right now. But I'm not sorry for kissing her tonight, for telling her I love her.

"Don't look at her like that!" Oliver snaps. Alex smiles gently then turns to face her father again.

"I don't expect you to understand right now, and I know this is going to take some getting used to, but I know you love me. And I know you love Elijah. Isn't that enough for now?"

Stephanie steps up and lays a hand on Oliver's shoulder. "You wanted Alex to find someone good, someone worthy of her. Elijah is someone good, Oliver. He's your friend, so you know what kind of man he is."

The air around us goes heavy with silence, and for a moment, I think that this is it. This is the end of my friendship with Oliver, the end of my job and life as I know it. But then Alex rests her head against my shoulder, and warmth fills my body along with a knowingness I can't explain. It tells me that as long as I have her, nothing is the end. Everything is a beginning.

"You really love each other?" Oliver asks, his voice resigned.

Alex looks up at me, her green eyes wide and hopeful. I kiss the crown of her head, and she exhales a happy sound before meeting her father's gaze. "Yes, Dad. I love Elijah."

"And I love Alex," I confirm. The weight of our words hang in the air.

Oliver presses his lips together and sticks his hands in his pockets. "I need some time."

"That's understandable," I say. "Just know that I won't do anything to hurt Alex. At least not intentionally," I swear. "And I really didn't do this to hurt you, Ollie. I care about your daughter. I care about you."

He searches my eyes for a lie before he expels a long sigh. "I know." He clears his throat. "I'm going to head home; I need to process this."

I nod at my longtime friend, knowing there isn't much else I can say right now. When Oliver's eyes meet Alex's, she steps out of my embrace and pulls her father into her arms.

She hugs him tightly. "I love you."

"I love you, too." Then he pulls back and grabs Stephanie's hand. "Call me tomorrow," he says to Alex. "And I'll see you on Monday, Astor."

He turns on his heel, and Stephanie looks at us over her shoulder with a broad smile. She makes the "call me" motion to Alex before they step back inside, which has us both chuckling quietly.

When they're safely out of sight, I tug Alex into my arms and rest my chin on her head, taking in her scent, her warmth.

"Tell me you love me again," she murmurs against my chest.

"I love you, Alex."

She hums, kissing the space over my heart. "I love you, too, Elijah."

Epilogue

ALEX

ONE YEAR LATER

"Oh my god, baby. I'm so proud of you!" I jump up and down as I hold Elijah's book in my hands.

He grins at me from his seat at the dining table, pulling me into his lap so he can kiss me soundly on the lips. "It's all thanks to you."

I shake my head. "No. You did this!" I say, turning the book over to see his picture on the back. "You made this happen."

He rests his head on my shoulder as I flip through the pages.

"My husband, the thriller author," I muse.

"Self-published author." He chuckles.

"Exactly, my husband, the author."

Elijah pulls the book from me and sets it on the table, holding my hands in his before kissing them. He takes extra time to place a kiss on the princess-cut diamond ring and matching wedding band on my finger.

"I love you, wife," he says, his blue eyes shining.

I press my lips to his, showing him my love as I open my mouth to his tongue, letting him kiss me deeply. When I pull back, I run my finger down his neatly trimmed beard then tug on it gently. "I have an anniversary present for you."

"Oh?" he asks, his brow shooting up.

Today happens to be the one-year anniversary of us officially getting together and the three-month anniversary of us getting married. What can I say? We like celebrating whenever we have a chance. Especially when we can escape to our favorite place—the lake house—to do so.

"I had my IUD removed," I say, cupping his cheek.

Elijah's cock jumps under my bottom, and I chuckle at his immediate reaction. But then his brow pinches.

"When?" he asks. "I would have gone with you to the appointment."

I roll my eyes at him, smoothing his brow with my thumb as I like to do. "It's fine, Mr. Serious. I wanted to surprise you."

He tucks a strand of my hair behind my ear. "Consider me surprised."

I hover my lips over his, then I grind my ass into his growing erection. "What do you say to putting a baby in me...*Daddy*?"

Elijah's eyes darken. I've never used that term with him before. It's never felt right, never felt not weird. Especially considering his relationship with my own dad. But I don't know, maybe it's the fact Elijah and I are married now. My dad has gotten over our relationship, or at least he's gotten used to and even likes the fact that Elijah and I are together, but—it feels right now. Especially since I plan on making him a daddy to several little red-headed babies.

Elijah grips my waist, his cock fully hard underneath me now. "You really mean it, Alex? You're ready to start a family?"

I nod. "Things have settled now with your work, and your book is out. Plus, my dad likes you again." That makes us both laugh. "I think it's time, don't you?"

He runs his thumb over the apple of my cheek, his pupils dilating as I squirm on his lap. "Is my dirty girl impatient?" He smirks.

His words make my thighs clench together, and I bite my lip, nodding. "I need you inside me, Elijah. I need to feel you fill me up. Make me yours."

The pad of his thumb traces my lower lip. "You are mine, Alex. You've always been mine."

"Then show me. Get me pregnant."

With a growl, Elijah lifts me off his lap, and before I know it, my back is on the dining room table. His book thumps to the ground.

"Elijah!" I cry, but it's as if my words have made him a man possessed. He pulls me by my thighs down the cool wood so my ass is at the edge. The table creaks when he bunches my green sundress up to my hips.

"You are a dirty girl," he chuckles playfully, his gaze between my legs at my naked pussy. It's already dripping with need for him, just like it always is.

He works his hand up and down my thighs in a soothing motion. "Now take out your breasts and play with your nipples. Show me what I own."

I whimper, the command in his voice making me wetter. Thankfully, my sundress has a low scooped neckline with a built-in bra so it's easy for me to shove it down. When I do, the elastic gathers underneath my breasts to push them up, giving Elijah a nice show as I trace a finger over my nipples and start to tease them.

"Good girl," he croons. "Now lay your head back, and keep doing that. Get your nipples nice and hard for me." With a small groan, I lay my head against the table and do as he asks, the sound of his belt buckle jingling and his clothes being removed turning me on even more. After a quick moment, he's standing over me again, completely nude. His lean muscled body is on full display.

"How do you feel, Alex?" he asks, his fingers gently brushing over the skin of my knees and thighs. He gets close to my pussy before he drags them back down again.

"Like I need you to fuck me," I say, my voice almost pleading.

His knuckle brushes over my mound, then he pulls back. "Hold open your legs for me."

I remove my hands from my breasts, bringing my legs up so I can loop my forearms under my knees and let my thighs part.

"Wider, wife," Elijah tsks. "I want you spread all the way open for me. I want to see your greedy cunt begging for my cock."

I moan, positive my arousal is dripping onto the table now. Over the last year, Elijah has gotten very, very good at giving me what I like, what I crave. He knows exactly what to do and say to make me absolutely crazy.

"That's my dirty girl," he praises, moving between my legs. He's pumping his cock now, a tiny bit of pre-cum dripping from the head. Before I can ask, he swipes it with his thumb then leans forward, dragging it across my lips so I can taste the bit of salty liquid.

He grins at me as I lap it up. Then he trails his hand back down toward my pussy, making sure to tweak my nipples and trace his favorite constellations of freckles on the available skin as he goes. By the time he reaches my clit, I'm practically weeping for him to touch me, to fuck me hard until I see stars behind my eyelids.

With one hand on my low belly and the other on his cock, he drags his swollen head up and down my slit, dipping it into my entrance to tease me before pulling back.

"Elijah," I cry. "Please, give me your cock. Let me milk you dry, Daddy."

A curse leaves his mouth, and he plunges inside me, the table creaking as he bottoms out with one single stroke. His balls slap against my skin.

"Fuck, Alex." He groans. "You make me so crazy."

He thrusts in again, his hands palming my heavy breasts. He's gripping them so hard it hurts, but in a good way, as he continues to fuck himself deeper into my pussy.

"Feeling's mutual," I cry as he hits my G-spot.

"You're mine, Alex." He drives into me harder. "Say you're mine."

"I'm yours, Elijah. I've always been yours." Unable to hold my legs up any longer, I wrap them around his waist, digging my heels into his ass so that he's buried even deeper inside me. "Yes, Daddy. Yes, yes, yes!"

He pounds into me furiously, his thrusts only seeming to get deeper as the table moves beneath us. It creaks to the point I wonder if we're going to break it, but I can't find it in myself to care.

"God, Alex. You're so tight, so wet. I can feel you gripping me. You feel so goddamn good," he says in a pinched voice, one that tells me he's close.

I clench my inner walls around him as hard as I can, and he swears. I'm desperate for him now, desperate to feel his release. I need him to plant his cum so deep in my womb that my body has no choice but to give me his babies. I know it doesn't work like that, but the idea is sexy.

"Come, Elijah," I plead, digging my nails into his waist. "I need you to fill me up. I need to feel your cum inside me."

"Such"—*thrust*—"a"—*thrust*—"dirty"—*thrust*—"girl," he grunts, lifting himself enough so that he can slide one of his hands down to rub my clit.

My body tenses the moment he touches my overly sensitive skin, and with another circle of his fingers, I'm orgasming underneath him, my vision blacking out as I arch off the table. I hold on to Elijah for dear life, using him as my anchor to reality as he keeps thrusting into me.

"Alex!" he cries, my pussy fluttering, gripping his cock as I ride my release. He grunts and drops his forehead against mine, and then, with a final plunge, I feel him tense. The moment his cum explodes inside me, I can't stop the second orgasm that overtakes me, helped along by his fingers that are still moving on my clit.

I cry out in pure ecstasy as I stare into Elijah's blue eyes, the eyes of my husband, the man I love. He continues to pump inside me, his release filling me just as I wanted. I lift my head to kiss him before squeezing my muscles around his dick, wanting every drop of cum.

When we both can't take anymore, our bodies spent, Elijah tucks a sweaty strand of hair behind my ear, and the table creaks again. A laugh bubbles out of me, and I cup his bearded cheek. "We should probably get up before we break the table."

Elijah huffs. "I'll buy a new one." He strokes his knuckles over my heated cheek, our bodies still connected. I can already feel his release leaking out of me, and I take comfort in the feeling of it. I know our first time since I got my IUD removed probably won't get us pregnant, but I'm hoping it will anyway.

When the table groans again, Elijah sighs and finally pulls out. But he doesn't let me up at first, instead standing back and staring at me, my legs splayed open with the mess of him between them.

"Beautiful," he murmurs. He steps forward to swipe his fingers through his release, pushing it back inside my pussy with a sly grin. He even holds his hand over my entrance for a moment so it doesn't slip out. When he's satisfied, he kisses up my legs and lower abdomen before placing several on my belly. The action does more to me than words ever could, and he knows it.

When he pulls back, he tugs me up off the table, pressing a slow and intimate kiss to my lips. Then he cups my cheek and stares into my eyes with more love than I ever thought someone was capable of showing.

"Thank you for loving me, Alex," he says after a moment. "And thank you for asking me to stay."

Tears cloud my vision, and I hug my husband to my body, pressing a kiss over his heart. "Thank you for staying," I whisper. "I love you, Elijah."

"I love you, too." Then he kisses me once more, and I melt into his lips, knowing that this is the start of our happily ever after.

Acknowledgments

WE DID IT! WE PUBLISHED ANOTHER BOOK! I say "we" because it takes a literal village to publish a book.

Now for another quick and dirty list of everyone who made this book possible!

First and foremost, I have to thank my readers, my street team, my beta team, and my ARC Team. Without you, I wouldn't be able to write another book. I wouldn't be here right now. Thank you for loving my plus-size babes. Thank you for giving me the opportunity to share my stories with the world. Thank you for sharing my voice with others.

I would also like to thank my friend and fellow author, Nicole Reeves, for always being there to talk me off a ledge. For being there to help me write this book. To bounce ideas off of and much more. Your support and love is integral to my success. I love you!

And a special shoutout to my Kaylaholics Facebook group members. Thank you for encouraging me to write Alex and Elijah's story. You wanted this book, you asked for this book, and I wouldn't have had the courage to write it without you. Also, thanks for helping me with the killer playlist!

I also have to thank all my beta and sensitivity readers individually: Suzi, Bailey, Mel, Jacqueline, Brianna, Jesenia, Dallas, Blair, Tyara, Alex, and Kasandra. Thank you for your love and valuable feedback. Especially on the kink elements of this book!

Thank you to Melissa Frey for editing another book of mine. You ROCK. Thank you for polishing up this story and making it the best it can be.

And I can't forget my friend and reader Brenna Jones for killing it with the discreet cover of this book and cheering me on, I'm so glad the internet brought me to you!

Lastly, thank you to Grayson Owens and Victoria Connolly for listening to me blab about my book and agreeing to bring Alex and Elijah to life via audiobook. You both have my heart forever.

Thank you for reading. Till next time...

Xoxo,
Kayla

P.S. Thank you to my Patreon members, Jackie, Kaitlyn, Jenn, Lindsey, and Kassandra. Your love and support means the world to me. Thank you for being part of The House of Smut and loving my plus-size babes.

Want More Alex & Elijah?
Get Their Bonus Chapter at www.patreon.com/kaylagrosse

More Books by Kayla Grosse

TRICK SHOT (BROTHER PUCKERS BOOK #1)
a spicy MMF novella with a plus-size female lead and male
lead...and their hot hockey player

PUCK SHY (BROTHER PUCKERS BOOK #2)
a spicy novella with a plus-size female lead and her golden
retriever hockey player

REIN ME IN (THE COWBOYS OF NIGHT HAWK #1)
a late brother's best friend, small town, cowboy romance with a
plus-size cowgirl

ROPE ME IN (THE COWBOYS OF NIGHT HAWK #2)
Available July 17th, 2024
a small town, country boy meets city girl romance with a
plus-size female lead

I LIKE YOU LIKE THAT
a second chance, rock star romance with a plus-size female lead

JUST AXE
Available November 4th, 2024
a super spicy MMF snowed-in lumbersnack romance

FALLING FOR THE MANNY
a single mom, contemporary romance by author duo Kayla
Nicole

For Exclusive Bonus Stories, Artwork, and More Visit:
www.patreon.com/kaylagrosse

Find Kayla:

Website: www.kaylagrosse.com
Instagram: @kaylawriteslife
Facebook: Kaylaholics Facebook Group
TikTok: @kaylagrossewriter
Twitter: @kaylagrosse

Printed in Great Britain
by Amazon

42761140R00091